MW01537632

A FALLEN CROWN IN ANOTHER WORLD

Volume 1 Part 1: Away from Home

Contents

Third Edition foreword

I want to take the time to share with you some insight to the creation of this book's Third Edition. There are no spoilers here, but if this doesn't interest you, feel free to skip forward!

I think it's safe to say that most, if not all, authors and artists who have a passion to create always strive to make it the very best it can be. That is precisely why I decided previously to create the Second Edition. I know that some reviews can be harsh but I was fortunate enough to receive a blunt, but fair and true, review which led me to go back, revaluate, and improve "Away from Home."

This is the Third Edition and it contains two types of major changes. They are: an overall quality improvement; and fleshed out story. The former includes things such as grammar correction, clarity improvement, and consistency changes. The latter expands on certain aspects, which I felt were lacking, and also sets up future books.

The goals of the Third Edition are the same as the previous: to make reading easier and less tedious while introducing more of the world; to better prepare for future volumes; to improve the overall quality.

If you're a new reader, I hope you'll enjoy your first step into the world of A Fallen Crown! If you're a returning reader, thank you for your patience!

A huge thank you to my editor, Ms. Jessica Brister, for her work on Part 1! The quality of this Third Edition is far higher than I could ever accomplish on my own thanks to your expertise and creative feedback. And thank you for your patience during this process. It's truly been a pleasure working with you, and I hope to continue doing so in the future!

Enjoy!

Acknowledgements

The following is to my family, my friends, and all who I had the fortune of meeting while working on my first novel. Your support means the world and helps drive me forward to improve as an author.

Furthermore, I would like to take this opportunity to express my sincere gratitude to those who played a major part in the development of A Fallen Crown.

To my unknown critic: If you, somehow, are reading this then I want you to know your criticism of the First Edition is greatly appreciated. Although it's never easy to hear the flaws of something you've spent so many, many hours working on, it's certainly just as important as being praised. I also appreciate the way you brought it up: respectful and aiming to help. If I could, I would refer to you directly. Unfortunately, your review went missing. So, thank you!

To Sam Koumi: Your feedback and insight in the past were much appreciated and something I still consider today as I continue to improve my craft. Your efforts in helping me improve the First Edition have not been forgotten, and I look forward to working with you in the future!

To Asu: Asu, you have without a doubt been the one who contributed the most to the development of the story. I was surprised by how committed you were to A Fallen Crown and how close your passion for world-building and storytelling came to my own. I feel like if the day would come where no one would read any of my work, you would be the last person there, stubbornly sticking by until the very end.

To Kairui-chan: It's difficult for me to put into words just how much I appreciate your work and talent, but I'll do my best. When I need the inspiration to write, I find myself often just staring at the cover art you made and have the world play in my mind. A Fallen Crown is my world, and your art is a beautiful rendition of it. I would love to continue working with you in the future. Thank you so much.

On grey, rainy mornings,
all you need to do is get up.

Chapter 1.

"Away from Home"

Lye 13 416

"CATHERINE!!" a boy's voice cried out as he shot up out of his bed. A pair of hazel brown eyes peeked out behind his messy dark hair; his eyes were wide open in fear and panic. A few seconds passed until the boy in ragged clothing became aware of his surroundings—that he was somewhere completely unknown. He was in a spacious but empty room. The only decorations around were some old, rustic beds with wooden bedside tables between them. The midday sun's light peeked in through windows and warmed up an otherwise cold room. His face turned pale.

"Where am I?" the boy thought, confused and with rapid, irregular breathing. A burning pain crept up his right arm that forced his eyes to look down. Extensive, intensely red wounds covered his skin and reached out to his fingers from his thumb to middle finger.

The loud crash of something brittle came from the hallway outside the room. It was followed by rapid footsteps.

"Frey?!" the voice of a girl shouted. It was immediately followed by the owner in the door who remained in disbelief. Her worried, bright blue eyes met the boy's. Like him, she too was dressed in an old, worn-down dress. Her golden blonde hair was chaotically tied up into a ponytail and still reached down to her neck while her face was neatly framed by locks of hair down each side of her face with side-swept fringes. Overjoyed and relieved beyond belief, she ran up to him and embraced him tightly. A pain shot through the boy's body, and he groaned loudly in response. "I'm sorry. I'm so sorry! I completely forgot!" she apologised after letting go.

The hurt subsided and instead turned into the lingering burn he felt earlier, though it soon became overshadowed by terror as another realisation dawned on him.

"*'Frey'? She was talking to me? No, it can't be... Did I?*" the boy thought and looked down at his trembling hands.

"Frey? What's wrong?" the girl asked anxiously when she noticed his odd behaviour.

The boy did not answer. "*I– I don't understand. How am I alive? Where am I? Catherine? Lynnea? I... can't sense them at all. No, wait...!*" he thought and quickly pulled up his shirt, the pain for a moment numbed by obsession. "*Nothing, just these strange wounds? Maybe I— No... No. I know that treacherous bastard pierced my stomach with that accursed sword...*" He leaned back and shut his eyes tightly as a deep sadness washed over him. With deep, shaky breaths and countless thoughts that ran through his mind, his hand gripped the bed sheet in an iron grip. "*I did... I died after all.*"

Frey, as he was referred to by the girl, had taken some time to calm his nerves while she sat next to him in complete silence. Because he had been searching for something that was not there, the young girl wondered if there was something she missed. Subtly, she looked around the room before she turned back to him.

"You're acting strange. What's wrong?" the girl asked hesitantly.

Again, the boy remained silent. "*This body isn't mine. Could it be Cyra's doing? Well, whoever it belonged to, it seems he was dear to this girl,*" he thought and looked at his visitor. He sighed – aware, despite his worries, of how she might feel from the words about to leave his lips. Softly, he asked, "I'm sorry, but who are you?"

The girl froze; her mouth opened slightly as if words wanted to come out but were lost before they could.

"Huh...? I–," her trembling voice said. With an

uncertain smile and a short, nervous laugh, she asked, "What do you mean 'Who am I?' You're joking, right?"

Frey shook his head. "No. I'm sorry."

The girl's face tensed. Her smile ran away from her face. At a loss, she hung her head, and parts of her face were obscured by hair. She got up without a word and left the room with slow steps. She disappeared down the hallway. There was a short period of silence before the creaking sound of a door opening and closing was heard. During this, though he pitied her, Frey said not a word.

Again, Frey was left alone with his thoughts. *"This would be unbelievable had I not known better. I died. I definitely did, yet I'm alive. That's a Servant's power for you. No wonder some were worshipped,"* he pondered with bittersweet amazement. He turned around to try to catch a glimpse of the outside but was stopped by a near unbearable agony. He grimaced as he sat back down. *"Some questions still remain. Where am I, and why can't I sense either Katja or Lynn?"* the boy thought as his eyes dotted from one part of the room to the other. The ever-present pain in his right arm drew his attention. Upon closer inspection, he saw clearly how the bright red wound covered most of his right arm and hand as it sprawled out in a strange-looking pattern. It ached terribly with each heartbeat; it felt like the wound itself could crack open at any moment – and as if a fire raged beneath his skin.

Some time passed before Frey heard the sound of a door opening again.

"Is that so? Frey finally woke up?" the voice of an older woman asked tiredly. The woman appeared in the doorway, garbed in a long, brown dress. Her hair was short and frizzy, and its grey colour testified to her old age. Her wrinkly lips curled up in a smile, and her eyes lit up with joy seeing Frey awake in his bed. She made her way to his bed with slow steps, all while the girl hid behind her. "Oh, Frey! I'm so happy to see you awake again! How are you?" she said delighted, though a bit tired, and sat down next to him.

"My arm hurts a lot. Otherwise, I'm okay. Thank you," Frey stated politely. He mustered all his strength to speak properly and not to groan in pain.

"I'll get on it! Before I do, though… My dear, do you remember either of us?" the grandmotherly figure asked as she leaned in closer and watched him carefully.

The boy looked at them both closely, trying to remember even the faintest thing. *"They seem familiar, but I can't tell if I've ever met them before. I guess it doesn't matter. If we knew each other, they certainly wouldn't be calling me Frey,"* he deduced before answering. "No. I'm sorry. I don't. Who are you? What happened to me?"

The old lady sighed after a few seconds, saddened by his response.

"It appears you have indeed forgotten," she mumbled worriedly. "I'll tell you what I know. I'm sure you must feel very lost right now."

"You have no idea…" Frey thought.

"Nearly a week ago, you were out on the grass fields with Alva here," the old lady said and gestured at the girl, who sat in silence at the end of his bed. "From what I understand, you were heading back here after collecting some plants for me. Suddenly, lightning struck you. You passed out, and Alva came running to our village for help. You've been unconscious until now," she explained. Her brows furrowed, and she quietly remarked, "There wasn't a single cloud in the sky that day. Where could it have come from…?"

"A lightning strike? That would explain why I look like this. Ah, damn it. It hurts so much! I hope it can be relieved," Frey thought, his jaw clenched in pain. "Sorry, uhm, miss…?"

"Carolia, dear! I've taken care of you here at the orphanage ever since you were little," the woman said and introduced herself with a familiar smile.

"Carolia," Frey repeated. "Do you have anything to help soothe the pain? I think it's getting worse," he said and hovered his left hand over his right.

"Yes, of course! I have just the herbs for the job! It will take a short while, but I'll try to hurry!" Carolia replied. She promptly shot up out of bed and left the two on their own.

Saddened and confused, Alva stared down at the floor for a while. Though the initial shock had passed, part of her did not want to give up hope that he had forgotten her.

"Frey…" she said somberly, "do you really not remember me?"

Although she tried her best not to sound or look too devastated by having been forgotten, the uncertainty in her voice was clear as day.

"This person was important to her. I could tell her what she wants to hear, but what would I say? And what good would it do?" Frey reasoned. "I'm really sorry. I don't remember."

"I see…" she said with disappointment written all over her face. Dismayed, her eyes could not bear to look into his.

"She took it pretty hard. Then again, what else could you expect? Maybe I should ask some questions to help take her mind off things. At the very least, maybe I'll learn more about where I am?" Frey silently reasoned. "Hey, Alva. My name is Frey, right? Could you tell me how old I am?"

When his voice called her name, she snapped out of whatever thought she was in.

Alva looked up. "Yeah, sure. You're fourteen. Actually, you just turned fourteen not too long ago! I'm still thirteen, so you're older than me but just by a *little* bit!" she told him with a hint of a smile.

"Geez, I'm a teen again?" Frey thought and threw his head back, though he regretted the motion immediately. *"Ow-ow-ow! I can't even move in the slightest. Well, a teen, huh…?*

At least this time it can't possibly be any worse than before – I hope." He sat back up and continued to ask, "When is my birthday?"

Alva hummed as she recalled the dates. "Let's see. Today is the 13th of Lye. Your birthday was on the 26th of Nirian, which was, um, twenty days ago… My birthday is on the 1st of Lyra, so that's another twenty days!"

Frey's eyes widened, and his mouth opened slightly in fear of a terrifying possibility.

"Nirian, Lyra? These aren't imperial standard calendar months. Aside from that, the dates don't match up either. What if… no!" Frey thought as his heart began to race. He forced a smile. "Forty days? You're right. That's hardly anything!" he said and laughed lightly.

Frey hesitated, unsure whether he wanted to hear the answer to his next question.

"What year is it?"

"The year? You don't even remember that? It's 416," Alva answered.

Time came to a grinding halt when she spoke the words aloud. Lightheaded, Frey sunk his head into the straw pillow with his eyes fixed at the ceiling. The pain in his arm faded away as his vision darkened. 'Year 416' endlessly repeated in his mind.

"416, Nirian, Frey. Doesn't take a genius to figure out what's happened. This isn't even my world. Ahhh, really?! Cyra was always such a pain to put up with, but how could she possibly have messed up like this? Wait, what if it wasn't a mistake? Could it be that she sent me here on purpose? But why would that be? I… I don't understand."

Though he had many questions that needed to be answered, he soon came to terms with the fact that they would remain unanswered – for now. With partially regained composure, he sat back up, determined to know more. While

Alva was bewildered by his strange reaction, she acted as if she paid it no attention.

"So, where are we? What is this place?" Frey asked in a friendly manner.

"You're in Delera village. Delera is part of the kingdom of Vallendar. And, um… Vallendar is pretty far north in Setura, at least from what I could tell on our maps!" Alva told him, now a little happier than before. A smile tugged on the corner of her mouth. "I know foreigners think Vallendar as cold, but I kinda like it!

"*Setura? That must be the name of this planet—maybe. Just to be sure, though,*" Frey thought before he asked, "What exactly is Setura?"

"What is Setura…? How do I answer that?" she mumbled with a brief, uncertain laugh. "The world, I guess!"

"Okay, so Setura's our world. It's a nice name," Frey remarked.

"Oh, right!" Alva said, having suddenly remembered something. "Granny has some maps in her office. If you'd like, I can bring one to show you what Vallendar looks like?"

Alva spoke enthusiastically and had brightened up much more than before as if her worries had been forgotten, even if just for a moment.

"Would you? I admit I'm a little interested," Frey answered. It appeared to him that Alva either enjoyed teaching or was simply happy to help him.

The girl stood up and nearly flew out the door without hesitation, more than eager to help.

Frey sighed once she left. "*It must be hard dealing with someone who doesn't remember you. I don't know what I'd do if it happened to Katja or Lynn… There isn't anyone else here either. Although Carolia treats us like family, I – or rather, Frey – appears to be her only friend. I can't imagine what she's feeling,*" he thought as he looked around the room.

There was no trace of anyone else who might have stayed there, save for himself, Alva, and Carolia. Out of the many beds in the room, the only ones made were his and, what Frey presumed to be, Alva's.

"Lonely, huh… I don't think I've ever felt this lonely myself. Luckily enough, I've ended up in the care of these kind strangers. Who knows where else I could have woken up? But–."

An image flashed through Frey's mind: Two young women with long, silver hair in elegant dresses laid motionless in crimson red pools. Despite their faces hidden behind hair, he felt their pleading stares all the same and was overcome by a sense of despair. He choked up and struggled to breathe as he forced back the tears.

"Catherine, Lynnea… I'm sorry."

A few minutes had passed when Alva returned with a rolled-up scroll in her hands. Initially excited, she abruptly stopped by the door. Still unnoticed, she stared at Frey, lost in thought, from a distance. Others may not have noticed it at first, but Alva somehow clearly saw the pain behind his vacant eyes and oddly indifferent expression. After a moment of hesitation, she eventually decided to walk up to him.

"Frey?" Alva asked with a gentle, soft voice and worried eyes. Frey blinked; a tear rolled down from the corner of his eye. She fetched him a piece of cloth from the bedside table by her own bed and dried his tear.

"Thanks…" he said quietly.

"What's wrong? Is it your arm?"

"No, I–," Frey stumbled over his words. He took a deep breath before he tried again. "When I woke up, it was from a nightmare. It was… terrifying. It's like I lost something important, and it seemed so real. Even now, I can't get it out of my head," he explained without revealing too much.

"I get it, must have been really bad. When I heard you

scream earlier… my legs wouldn't move for a few seconds. Did that have something to do with it? What was it, something like 'Cath–?'"

"YES!" Frey shouted angrily.

Alva jumped out of fright from his sudden hostility, and Frey immediately caught onto his unwarranted reaction.

"Sorry! Sorry, I didn't mean to shout. I don't know what flew into me," Frey apologised profusely.

Though he said that, Frey was well aware of why he had lashed out at her. As the eldest brother, he was the one to go to when his younger sisters needed help. Though a tiring and mostly thankless job, he held it dearly. To hear someone else speak their name when he had not yet come to terms with reality caused him to lose his temper.

"No, no, it's okay. Maybe I shouldn't have asked," Alva told him with a faint, forced smile. She lifted the scroll in her hands in an attempt to switch the subject. "I brought the map. Do you want to look at it?"

"No, I suddenly feel tired. Sorry for having you go get it. Maybe later," he said in a low tone as he averted his eyes and wearily leaned back against the propped-up pillow.

"That's all right. I'll leave you alone, so you can get some rest. Maybe there's something I can help within the kitchen?" Alva said and smiled so that he would not think her to be hurt. Though unsure whether to go or not, she figured it was best to give him some space and neatly tucked away the map under a strap around her waist, and left.

Back on his own, Frey's thoughts were drawn to what he saw.

"I wonder if that was real or if it was my imagination. No, it's real. I know it was… I know. It just happened, but why does it feel like it was long ago? Not that it changes anything. We died, and now here I am on my own. I can't sense Catherine or Lynnea at all. I don't even know if I can use my

magic. *Damn that Servant! Why?! Why did she save me? Why not them?!*" Frey thought and slammed his right fist in the bed. A sharp pain shot through his arm and chest when he struck the bed twice more. It hurt enough to pause his breathing for a few seconds. He closed his eyes shut. "*Why not them…? I'm sorry Katja, Lynn. I failed you.*"

Minutes later, Alva returned with Carolia. By now, Frey had succeeded in calming his nerves.

"Sorry for the wait, dear," Carolia said as she stepped through the door. In one hand, she held a mortar and pestle filled with red paste and in the other a clear glass flask. "I tried to finish up as soon as possible, Frey. I know it must ache a lot."

Frey opened his eyes and straightened up. "It's not too bad when nothing's touching it."

"This salve I have is made from a plant called Sorellia. I used it to treat you while you were unconscious. It numbs pain and helps your body heal. Applying it will hurt, but it should last a day or two," she explained as she sat down on the chair by his bed. Alva sat down on the other side of him.

"I'll put up with it as long as it works," Frey said and managed a half-smile.

"I also have this potion, courtesy of one of the mages who visited us with the Oracle. It's supposed to help you sleep. Take a sip if you feel that you need it," Carolia explained and put the flask on the bedside table.

"*Whoa-whoa-whoa! Wait one minute. Hold on! Potion, mages, the Oracle? There is magic here then?*" Frey thought, greatly surprised. "Carolia, did you say mages? As in, people who use magic?"

"You don't remember that either?"

"I told you, I don't think he remembers anything, Granny," Alva reminded her.

"I know, dear. I hoped he could recall something,"

Carolia acknowledged. "To answer your question, Frey: yes, mages use magic. Although it's not an ability everyone possesses, it's not a rare one either."

"What about the Oracle? Who's that?"

"A servant to the King, His Majesty Sebastian. Though she cannot use magic, she is a powerful seer. They say she can see the very soul of a human and even catch glimpses of the future," Carolia explained with mixed emotions. "I can't say I don't feel sorry for the poor girl, though... Such a young one, still but a child and already carrying such responsibility."

Frey was confused. "Why was she here?"

Alva looked away and stared out the open window. Even when Frey looked directly at her, she refused to meet his eyes.

"It was almost a year ago. It turns out that Alva here has the potential to become a mage. The Oracle said her soul was incredibly strong. With the right education, she could become a highly-skilled mage!" Carolia told him, full of pride, all while the girl herself intently stared out the window. Frey had a hunch as to why she did.

"Did I have any potential?" Frey asked, having guessed the answer.

Carolia held off and looked at Alva. The delicate old lady understood too late that she did not want him to know. Unfortunately, Frey had already asked, and Carolia did not want to lie to him.

"No. The Oracle said that she could see no such potential in you. It was only Alva who was invited to go with her to attend a good school. Of course, that would mean leaving us and our village for many years," Carolia told him. She gently laid her hand on Alva's knee with a comforting smile on her lips. "She didn't want to leave us."

"Is that so? To give up such an opportunity for a friend is noble. Perhaps a little foolish," Frey thought, yet he admired her.

"The Oracle is a clever girl," Carolia continued with a chuckle. "She knew and told us that she would wait one more year until Alva's fourteenth birthday to hear our answer. Her advisor strongly objected toward returning, but her word was final!"

"I will have made up my mind until then," Alva mumbled to herself and caught the attention of Carolia and Frey. "No matter what, I *will* choose!"

Alva's sudden outburst of confidence made them laugh, though it only made Frey's pain worse.

Frey instinctively reached for his arm but stopped before touching it. "Okay, Carolia, would you please? It's getting worse."

"Of course, my dear. Let's get right to it!" she replied and stood up.

After placing down the mortar and pestle on the side, she carefully lifted Frey's ragged shirt up and over his head with Alva's help. The lightning pattern became evident against the rest of his skin as it reached from the top of his chest, back, and right shoulder to the tip of his three damaged fingers. Although they took great care in applying it, the mere touch against the wounds was excruciating. He clenched his jaw and let out suppressed groans every once in a while.

"God, it feels like my skin's set on fire—or worse, like it's being burnt away! I– I think it's over soon," Frey thought when Carolia began to rub the salve on his hand.

They finished his treatment in a couple of minutes, and Frey sighed with relief as the pain began to fade away.

"Thank God… it's over!" Frey exclaimed. "How long until it starts taking effect?"

"It shouldn't be too long. It'll be a few more minutes until your skin starts to absorb it," Carolia told him and stood up, now with an emptied mortar in hand. "You'll have to excuse me, children, but there are some errands that need to be taken care of. If you need me for anything, just look down the road, Alva. I'll be back soon! And Frey, remember that you have your potion if you need to rest. The more you sleep, the better!" she told him firmly but lovingly in a way only a grandmother could. Frey nodded.

After the old lady had left, the young boy's stomach growled long and loudly.

Alva grinned. "You must be starving, Frey! You haven't had any real food in a while now. Lunch is almost ready, and I have some cleaning up to do in the kitchen. I'll be there until Granny's treatment starts to kick in. Then I'll help you get dressed. Sound good?" Alva asked, her caring voice smooth as silk.

Frey appreciated her actions. "That's fine. Also, Alva, thanks for your help. I mean it," he told her earnestly.

"Of course. Any time, Frey," she said with a smile and left.

The boy was impressed by her maturity and affection that she showed him despite their circumstances. *"Such a caring person. It kinda reminds me of– someone? Not sure who. Hm. Maybe I can trust her."*

As the sun's rays shined on Frey's bed and skin, a cold breeze swept through the room to hit his naked upper body. His arm numbed when the salve finally began to be absorbed through the skin. The searing pain turned into a tolerable sting and granted him a great sense of relief. However, when he tried to move his arm or fingers, he discovered that they barely responded.

Right on cue, Alva appeared in the doorway. "Hey, how are you feeling?"

"Way better!" Frey told her. "It's starting to work now. I can't move my arm that much, but it's not hurting as badly anymore."

Alva looked at him with some scepticism, worried he

hurt more than he let on. "As long as it's not too bad," she murmured and approached with a piece of fabric folded up in her hand. "I figured it was about time it gave effect. Carolia said that it's an excellent pain reliever but that it also has some paralysing properties."

"Just where it was applied, I hope?" Frey asked with a laugh.

"Yeah, it's not that strong!" Alva smiled.

"Anyway, since I'm feeling better now, do you still have the map? I wouldn't mind taking a look!" Frey asked, interested to learn about his location.

"Sure, I have it right here," she said and pulled it out from behind her back. "Are you sure you don't want to eat first, though?"

Frey's stomach rumbled loudly as if it answered the question for him. "No, you're right. I'm starving!" he laughed, embarrassed. "Where do we eat?"

"The kitchen is on the right, down the hall. I'll help you get on your feet after we get you dressed!"

Said and done. Alva helped Frey put his shirt back on and then unfolded the cloth she brought with her. She tightly tied each far corner together to form a rudimentary arm sling and carefully placed his arm in it. Then, they made their way to the kitchen together.

The orphanage's kitchen was spacious. It had a stove, a sink – with some sort of crystal embedded into the wall behind it – and a wide kitchen countertop with plenty of utensils, herbs, spices, and some cured meat laid out on top of it. On a sturdy table by a large window, there were three reddish-brown bowls and spoons laid out. By the kitchen door laid what remained of the brittle item that Frey heard break earlier.

When Frey stepped inside, his nose was filled with a fragrant, meaty scent that only made his stomach cry even louder. Alva helped him sit down on a bench by the table before she sat down on the other side. Loud crackling from inside the stove gave Frey a sense of nostalgia. It was comforting.

After a moment of silence, Frey asked, "Does Carolia cook?"

"Yup! She does the cooking most of the time. I usually help her prepare everything beforehand while I try to learn how to cook too!" Alva shared enthusiastically. "I hope someday to be as good at it as Granny. Don't know how she does it, but even something as simple as eggs taste amazing when she makes it!"

Frey found her childish excitement charming. "You really love food, huh?"

"Of course! You know I–." She stopped mid-sentence and shamefully looked down. "Sorry… I forgot that… you know."

"Try not to let it bother you. It's not like this is your fault," he told her in an attempt to lighten the mood.

Although she nodded in response to his reassurance, Alva remained uncomfortable. Not sure what to do or say, afraid to bring up his amnesia again, she nervously shifted around in her seat.

Frey exhaled, stood up, and walked over to the windowsill where he leaned on it with his healthy arm. Alva's eyes followed him closely. Just outside, a stone's throw away, was a bountiful vegetable farm. Past it, cattle grazed freely on far-stretching plains. In the distance, far away from the village, he spotted the white peaks of the Snowcrown Mountains creep up over the horizon.

"How beautiful. They would have loved this," Frey thought. The beauty of the land gave him butterflies. "Listen, Alva," he said calmly, "I don't know the Frey you do, and I don't know if there will ever be a time I will. And I know this is not what you want to hear, but who I am now is me, no one

else. I'm glad and grateful to be here, even if I still don't know exactly where that is or who I am. I feel lost and alone right now, but I still feel like you are someone I can trust."

Alva watched him speak; she listened carefully to every word spoken. The way he talked made her feel like no matter what, everything, somehow, would be okay. Still, one question remained with her.

"What makes you think that?"

Instead of replying immediately, Frey continued to observe the outside.

"There are a few reasons. If I were to name one that stood out, it would be your hesitation to go with the Oracle. To risk losing such an opportunity so that I wouldn't be left alone is a sign of compassion – especially when you have such a bright future ahead of you," Frey explained and expressed his feelings on the matter.

"I–… I didn't want to leave you. I felt like I would be abandoning you if I went with them," Alva said with a shaky voice.

"It's not an easy choice to make, but that's okay. Not all are," Frey told her.

"'Okay'?" Alva thought and hung her head. "It's not okay," she mumbled, her voice not any louder than a whisper.

Frey turned around. Concerned, he asked, "Alva?"

"It's not okay… because it feels like I'm alone here— like I'm talking to a stranger. And I hate it. I hate that feeling! Even with Granny, I feel so alone!" Alva told him as she kept raising her voice. She looked up with teary eyes to meet his. "I spent all day and every night waiting for you to wake up, not knowing if you ever would! Elder Rolan even said I shouldn't hope for too much. And when you finally woke up, it turns out you don't even remember who I am! Do you have any idea how it makes me feel?!" she shouted on the verge of tears. She crossed her arms over the table and buried her face to hide.

"And you're the reason why…" she whispered.

Frey stood speechless. Although he grew up having to deal with the tantrums of his sisters and believed he knew how to respond to her emotions, he instead became overwhelmed. He walked up to her to place his hand on her back but doubted himself and decided against it.

"I'm sorry. I didn't realise you felt this way," he said after a few moments.

"No! No. I should apologise," she sniffled and raised her head. "It's not your fault. I just… I don't know what to do." Tears rolled down her face and more fell when she tried to wipe them away.

Frey left the kitchen and came back with a piece of cloth in his hand. When he tried handing it over, Alva noticed it was the cloth that she had given to him earlier.

She looked up. "I didn't mean to yell at you. I shouldn't have. I'm sorry."

"Don't. It's fine," Frey told her with a warm look as his left hand dried her face.

"It's pretty childish of me to cry and scream, isn't it?" Alva asked with a short laugh, now a little more relieved.

"Not at all" Frey smiled and put down the cloth. "I don't even know how I would feel if I was in your situation. Besides, doesn't it feel better now?"

"A little. I still feel bad for screaming at you, though," she confessed, embarrassedly.

"*Although this life of poverty, at least by comparison, is vastly different from what I'm used to, when it comes down to it, we're no different. And to think some dared believe it to be so, just because of their wealth or lineage…*" Frey thought back to his past. "I'm here if you need to talk some more."

"No. I think I've already said what I needed to say. Even if it came out a little differently to what I think I wanted it to," Alva told him, surprised and a little ashamed by her behaviour.

"Sometimes, all you need is to speak directly from your heart. You feel better now. Isn't that what you said?"

"I did. But I didn't want to make it sound like I'm blaming you or anything. I really didn't," she clarified.

"Don't worry. I know! A person can only go around and carry so much before falling to their knees. That's when we tend to make mistakes—like saying or doing things we don't really mean," Frey added.

"Maybe… Thanks for understanding, Frey," Alva thanked him.

"Don't be silly. I was so obsessed with my worries that I forgot how much this affects you too. I should have known better," Frey said and went back to his seat. "To be honest with you, I don't really know what to do either. I feel lost and completely out of place. The only thing I can do now is to rely on you and Carolia. And if you let me, I promise that you can rely on me too. I won't let you down again."

"Frey, you didn't let me down. I–."

Frey raised his hand. "I did. I have no one else here. I have no excuse. I should have thought about your feelings earlier, but I didn't. It's shameful, and I'll make up for it if you let me," Frey promised her. *Wait, what am I even saying? Where is this coming from? Why am I getting worked up like this?*"

"*He… He still cares,*" Alva thought to herself. Although his behaviour was strange to himself, to Alva, his apparent honesty reminded her of the old Frey. Her eyes lit up, bright and clear.

Ever since he woke up, Frey had been under the impression that she had simply kept up appearances. It was the first time he saw a genuine smile on her lips. The worries and loneliness were no longer there. Alva shot up and almost ran around the table to hug him tightly. This time, there was no sound of pain.

"I'm sorry I doubted you. I won't anymore," she whispered with her face buried in Frey's shirt. It took him by surprise, and he felt happy for her. "You've been talking weirdly, but I know you still think and feel the same as you used to."

Frey said nothing but gently patted her back. "*In a place where so many had little choice but to sacrifice others just to survive, the three of us always dreamed that everyone help lift each other up rather than pushing them down. On the off chance that this boy felt the same way, then maybe Setura is worth staying in?*" Frey thought, uplifted by a peculiar sense of hope. While he knew the choice in staying was not up to him, at that moment, it did not matter.

Alva and Frey took deep breaths. Since his awakening, there had been constant tension in the air that was now mostly lifted. By the time Alva returned to her seat, Carolia appeared in the hallway to see them both in high spirits.

A wrinkly smile lit up her face, and she placed down a basket of eggs on the counter. "You seem much better now, Frey!"

"All thanks to your salve! It doesn't hurt at all anymore. That thing is incredible," Frey complimented her.

"Isn't it? The Sorellia plant, better known as a Demonshade, is quite remarkable. Although it can only grow in colder climates, it is quite a famous plant, popularised by Demonic Contractors because of their frequent use of it," Carolia explained as she placed down a woven basket on the countertop.

"Wait, Demonic Contractors? There are… demons?" Frey asked, surprised.

"Oh, yes! And spirits too! It's generally only mages who can bind them through contracts, although there are some exceptions," Carolia continued to tell him. She turned around and, to her surprise, was met by an awestruck Frey, who was not disturbed by the existence of demons in the slightest. "I can tell that you have many questions, but you'll have to wait until after lunch if you want to hear more. A better question is what you two were talking about before I came in?"

"Oh, that. It wasn't anything too important," Alva answered cheerfully. "I just got the chance to say what's been on my mind. But what's important is that Frey is still with us," she continued and threw an eye at Frey.

Frey nodded in agreement contentedly. Frey got back up and walked up to Carolia, who picked up eggs from the basket and cracked a few of them into a bowl. *"Eggs?"* he briefly thought, confused. Then, he spoke up. "Carolia, there was something I wanted to ask you; it's about the herbal treatment."

"Hm? What would that be?"

"Is herbalism common? If it is, where can you learn more about it?" Frey asked as he watched her pour the now beaten eggs into a sizzling hot iron pan.

Carolia raised her brow in surprise. "What? You're interested in herbalism? That's something new!" she exclaimed with a hearty laugh.

"I guess so—thanks to your salve. I thought it'd be a good idea to know some herbalism if I would ever need it again. I take it I wasn't very interested in this before?" Frey jokingly asked.

"You could say that! If I even so much as mentioned it, you were nowhere to be seen!" Carolia chuckled, joined in by Alva. "If you are now, I'll help you in whatever way I can. We have quite a good selection of books in my study. All you need to do is ask!"

"I'll remember that. Where did you learn it? Is there somewhere you studied?" Frey asked, eager to know.

"Not exactly, my dear, no. My grandmother was a skilled practitioner; she taught me all I know," Carolia explained, proud of the skills she inherited. "Unfortunately, I don't know of any place that teaches it the way alchemy is."

"Oh, how come? What's the difference?"

Carolia's bushy, grey brows furrowed while she took time to think of her answer as she placed the cooked eggs on a plate. "I suppose it's because alchemy is widely thought to be as capable as herbalism—but in a more potent form. That's not entirely true as certain properties of some plants are lost in the alchemical refinement process. Admittedly, potion brewing is far more convenient to carry, use, and be sold. It's ridiculous, though," Carolia shook her head. "The basics of alchemy are all derived from herbalism, yet schools refuse access to anyone not a mage!"

"I see…" Frey grumbled. "*If I had to guess, the reason is probably that there's far more money involved in alchemy. If true, then educating non-mages would use up more resources than it'd be worth. Anyway, that's enough questions. I'll make sure to keep an eye out for any books or lexicons that have to do with either.*"

"There is time for it later! How about you take a seat, dear? The food is just about ready," Carolia said and heaved the heavy pot off the stove.

Filled with beef, potatoes, carrots, and a lovely mix of herbs and spices, the scent filled Frey's nostrils and made his mouth water. She placed it down on the table with a thud and scooped up large portions of the bubbling stew, using a wooden ladle—each scoop full of lean cuts of meat, potato wedges, and colourful vegetables. The plate of scrambled eggs was given to Alva.

"Wait, what? You're having eggs with stew?" Frey asked, surprised.

"What's wrong with that? I told you her scrambled eggs are amazing. Hey, don't you judge me now! It's tasty!" she exclaimed in her defense, and with a spoon in hand pointed at him.

"Well, I suppose you like what you like," Frey conceded with a light chuckle.

With eyes set on the bowl before him, Frey could barely contain himself. On the first bite and when his teeth sunk into the tender meat, the flavours burst. Unable to resist any longer, he gave in and shovelled in spoon after spoon. Alva and Carolia stared at him with wide-open eyes when he finished his bowl in seconds. Finished, he leaned back contentedly.

"This must be what food in heaven tastes like," Frey thought as the stew heated up his body.

"My word, you've finished already? With an appetite like that, you'll recover in no time!" Carolia laughed joyously.

"It was amazing! Alva's right: you're an incredible cook, Carolia! Could I have some more?" he asked eagerly with the bowl in hand.

"Of course! Have as much as you want!" Carolia replied and stood up, happy to hear how much he loved it.

As Frey sat there and ate now at a much slower pace, he observed Alva and Carolia speak. The girl was like a completely different person, cheerful and with an illustrious aura around her. He glanced out the window.

"It's so peaceful here. I wouldn't mind if every day was like this until my last breath."

Indulged in the calm and quiet, Frey suddenly heard some strange, indistinguishable whispers. It came from neither Alva nor Carolia; it was a most unpleasant feeling.

"Brother..."

A chill ran down Frey's spine when the ghostly voice of a young woman called out for him: it was Lynnea. He leaned his head on his hand with an empty look on his face. In an instant, the comforting warmth was blown away by the wind.

Chapter 2.

"Two Friends"

Lye 30 416

A little over two weeks passed and spring had finally grasped its long-awaited hold on the land. During this time, Frey had done little more than eat or sleep while recovering. On his better days, Alva volunteered to teach him what she knew of magic, demons, and the world. One thing he learned after puzzling the information together was that while the number of days in a year was fewer in Setura, each day was longer than in his word—something he had not noticed until then.

The midday sun's rays found their way through gaps in the trees and created pillars of light down to the ground. With summer just around the corner, the spring air was filled with the scent of blooming flowers. Frey was no longer in need of the arm sling – or any other treatment for that matter – as his wounds had healed remarkably quick. He and Alva were tasked by Carolia to gather some ingredients in a nearby small forest for Carolia's herbalism. They had already gathered enough yellow tree moss and plenty of white tundra berries. All they were missing was a single black cap mushroom.

"Frey, I found it!" Alva's cheerful voice called from between the trees. "I found the black cap!"

"Great job, Alva! I'll be right there!" Frey shouted back. He made his way over to her with careful steps over roots and between rocks. Although his body had healed well and in turn left behind prominent scarring, he was worried about tripping and falling on it.

"That's the last thing on our list," Alva said when Frey arrived and tossed it in a basket. "We can take a break before we head back to the village. What do you think?"

"I don't think Carolia would mind. It's such a nice day after all," Frey replied as he looked around.

After a few minutes of wandering in search of a good place to rest, they came across a great oak tree tilted on a slope with massive roots that sprawled above the ground around its base. Alva and Frey sat down with their backs against its trunk, cradled between the roots—Alva higher up and Frey further down. A mild spring breeze brushed against their faces while they listened to the singing of spring birds.

"Thank the heavens. We can finally sit down and relax!" Alva said. She stretched and then exhaled sharply. "We finished up early today. You found the moss and berries almost instantly! I'm sure we would've been here forever otherwise!"

"It's all thanks to Carolia's instructions. Yellow tree moss needs plenty of moisture, so trees near springs or streams are the most promising. White tundra berries need a lot of nutrition and often push away other plants; they're easy to find in grassless glades. The mushrooms were the hardest to find since they prefer to grow in darker places and can hide nearly anywhere!" Frey explained.

"It's amazing how you remembered all that and what they look like when Granny only showed you once. I have to sit down and read something over and over again to remember it! Maybe because it's so boring," Alva laughed but immediately covered her mouth. "Oh, but don't tell Granny I said that…"

"I won't! Maybe," Frey answered jokingly.

A few minutes passed without either speaking.

"Hey, Frey," Alva said and broke the silence. She tilted her head back to stare up at the tree.

"What?" Frey casually replied with one arm covering his eyes.

"I've made up my mind," she told him.

"Oh? About what exactly?" Frey asked even though he knew what she meant. He lifted his arms slightly to peek up and to his left where Alva sat.

"I've decided to go with the Oracle."

"Really? How come?" Frey asked again with his curiosity well hidden.

"If the Oracle says I have potential, it means I can become strong, right?" Alva asked him.

"If you give it your all, I don't see why not," Frey told her.

"Then, if I'm strong, I can protect other people. Right?"

Frey turned silent. "The strength to protect, huh…" he muttered under his breath.

"What's that?" Alva called out.

Frey shook his head. "Sorry, just mumbling!" he quickly replied. "You're right, though. If you're strong, you can protect others. It's especially important in a world like ours," Frey told her. What he referred to was the wide range of creatures that inhabited Setura – creatures that were a mere work of fiction in Frey's world.

"Even if it's dangerous, I want to try. I know I can do it!" Alva proudly announced her intention to become a mage.

"Good, that's what I want to hear!" Frey said, glad for her sake. However, he knew well what work laid ahead of her. "As with anything, study and practice will not be easy. Even if you're talented, it means nothing if you don't take it seriously. There will also be times when you'll doubt yourself or question if what you're doing is really worth it. Your success will depend on whether you will be able to push on through," Frey told her as he stared off into the distance.

Alva peeked her head out over the roots above him and looked at him as if wondering how he could know about that.

"I-, uh, that's just what I think! Who knows? I could be completely wrong!" Frey said and looked up to her with an innocent smile. "Anyway," he continued," have you heard about the feral wolves? I talked to one of the guards yesterday, and they told me some interesting things. They're bigger and smarter than any normal wolf. I wouldn't want to meet one here…"

Alva froze. "Shut up! Don't say things like that when we're alone in a forest!" she shouted.

"Sorry. Sorry! You don't have to worry. They only live in huge forests! There's no way they would ever come here! Ours is way too tiny!" he assured her in an attempt to calm her down.

Alva sighed. "Try and think about what you say before opening that mouth of yours…" She frowned with arms crossed. "I don't want to hear things like that when we're on our own. What would you do if one showed up?"

"Not sure this fear will help if you might have to fight one someday," Frey thought. Still, he found her outburst endearing. "You're right. I'm sorry. You don't need to worry. I promise. They need a lot of living space—like the Enn forest—and are extremely territorial. They'd never leave it!"

"Even if I know I'll have to face things like that eventually, you can't just…" she mumbled, uncertain of herself.

Frey picked up on her fear. "I don't think you have anything to be afraid of," he told her with a gentle voice. "Everyone has their own challenges they must overcome one day; some are bigger, some smaller. If you ask me, all you have to do is remember why you're there in the first place. Is it to prove something to others, to yourself? Whatever it is, a reason is all you need to succeed."

"Is that enough?"

"Depends on the reason," Frey replied and laid back down. He took a moment to gather his thoughts. "Even if the ground crumbled under your feet or if the sun's warm light vanished, it would catch you before you fell and light up even the darkest day." He subtly glanced at her with a raised brow. "So, how much do you want to protect? That's your reason, isn't it?"

Alva said nothing and sat back down in deep thought. When she closed her eyes, she saw Frey and Carolia in the village and all the hardworking villagers who made sure their home could continue to be. All she could think of were the many years she spent growing up at the orphanage. Whenever a new child arrived, she was quick to make friends with them. But every time someone new came, they soon left for a new home. She always remained with her grandmother, year in and year out. For the longest time, she could never understand why they all left so soon. Then Frey arrived. As she thought back to her younger years, it felt as if it was only yesterday when they were kids and played together in the fields of the far-stretching plains or helped Carolia or the other villagers. Many memories were made in Delera, and the very thought of losing it made her sick to her stomach. Yet, another feeling welled up within: a burning desire to keep both Frey and the home they grew up in safe.

"I'll do it. If you and the Oracle think I can do it, I know everything will be fine. I promise I'll protect you and everyone else!" Alva proclaimed with brilliant confidence and unshakeable resolve.

Frey could not help but break a smile as her determination reminded him a lot of Catherine.

"You're going to protect me, huh?" Frey remarked with a chuckle.

Alva's cheeks turned rosy red. "W-w-what's wrong with that?!" she stuttered and shot out of her spot. Flustered, she glared at him. "You don't think I can or something?"

"No, no, that's not at all what I meant!" Frey laughed. "I just didn't expect you to mention me. That's all! Of course, I'm glad you did," he said merrily and looked up at her with a childish grin. Even though he teased her every chance he had, he truly appreciated the sentiment.

"Here I am trying to be considerate, and all you do is make fun of me! That's not very kind of you," she said and folded her arms while she pretended to be hurt. She opened one eye slightly to see if he felt bad.

Frey was not fooled. Instead, he found it endearing. *"Trying to guilt trip me, huh? Unfortunately for you, I grew up with two younger siblings!"* Frey thought and let out a small laugh. He straightened up and got a little more serious. "For what it's worth, I think this is a once-in-a-lifetime opportunity. I know you'll become an exceptional mage." He paused. "I'm sure there will be a lot of things for you to experience and many people to share them with – for better or for worse. Nevertheless, it will shape you into who you'll become. It'd be a shame to miss all that. Just imagine how many people would give anything, absolutely anything to be given the chance you have. Don't take it for granted!"

Alva never thought of it that way. Rather than seeing it as an opportunity, she feared leaving home. She knew little of what to expect once on her own, and it scared her. *"He's right. Both Granny and the Oracle said the same thing. There are so few who ever get handpicked by an Oracle, and so many of them found success – or so I've been told. I really can't let it go to waste."*

Frey noticed her stern face and did not want her to overthink it. "Either way, no matter what your final decision is, you'll have my full support."

"Thanks, Frey. It means a lot," she thanked him, now more at ease.

Frey leaned back down to stare up at the canopy. A faint, thunderous rumble echoed in the air. Out of the countless creatures inhabiting Setura, ranging from dreadful undead to the fickle giants to peaceful river serpents, one stood above all else.

"*Dragons… From what I've seen so far, this world isn't as advanced as mine. But what it lacks in technology, it more than makes up for it elsewhere. It's like straight out of a fantasy book! I'm living the dream of every adult and child who grew up on stories like the life here,*" Frey thought. Curious, he asked, "Say, Alva, would you ever want to meet a dragon?"

"HUH?!" Alva exclaimed, again forced out of her cradle to stare at him in disbelief. "Are you kidding?! What sane person would ever even want to get near them? You could hear the trembling metal from the new guards at the village every time they hear them roar!"

Frey ignored her worry. "I'd love to meet one! I feel like the legends and stories don't tell the whole truth. Carolia said that humans and dragons once were able to speak to one another and that there was even a point where we fought together! Just imagine the things they could teach us!" he said with unbridled enthusiasm. "What knowledge do they have that we don't? What can we discover about magic and our history? It drives me crazy just thinking about it! Ahhh!" he rambled and ruffled his hair. The passion to seek out new knowledge was something he always had expressed. It was not often he showed strong emotions about anything, except when it came to his family. This was true in both his current life and his past.

Alva burst out laughing. "You're insane! They would swallow you whole before you could even say a word! Even if we could speak to them, why would they tell us anything after the war?"

As Frey had mentioned, there was a time where dragons and humans fought together in what was known as the Dusk War. However, at some point following the end of the war, something happened that caused a brief but devastating conflict between the two sides, though what exactly no one seemed to know.

Frey, not used to be laughed at, glared at Alva. Alva noticed his unamused gaze, though she only laughed harder when she tried to stop.

Unappreciated, Frey continued to speak. "If you think about it this way: why have the dragons not attacked anyone? You can hear and see them all the time, yet they've not once touched a village or killed a human. Doesn't that make you wonder why?" Frey asked her. His reasoning was fair, and Alva stopped laughing. "If they are those hideous, ravaging monsters told in hundreds of stories, how come they've left us alone? We're right here, near the mountains. Surely they could wipe us out in a day if they wanted to?"

Alva thought about what he pointed out. "Hm, okay. I see where you're coming from, Frey. Maybe they just don't think it's worth the effort?"

"Maybe…" Frey mumbled. "Regardless, I don't think they're stupid creatures. People say that they've been here long before we even existed and that we once fought as allies. They're intelligent. I just know it. I believe that as long as you don't give them a reason to kill you, you should be safe to meet with them."

It was only then that Alva realised how interested Frey was in them. She crossed her arms and leaned over the branch. "Well, fine. Even if you're right, how would you meet one? Would you just try and walk up to one and start talking to it? Doesn't seem very likely, does it?" Alva asked and rested her head on her crossed arms.

Frey's face lit up like the sun. "That's… exactly what I'd do! What a great idea!" he exclaimed as if it was a given he would meet one.

"Yeah, yeah. Sure, you'll do that. I believe it," Alva waved away his brashness.

"You don't even pretend like you mean it…" Frey said and mimicked Alva with crossed arms. She stared at him while he looked away, pretending to be hurt by her lack of faith. He caught her eyes, and then they both burst out into laughter.

"Yeah, as if I would buy that!" she told him with teary eyes. She never thought he could act that way.

As they calmed down, they sank back into the comfortable holes between the tree roots. Frey thought back to the weeks that had passed and of how Alva had come to accept things as they were.

"*I suppose it wouldn't be that strange to be a little different if you one day woke up and all your memories were gone. The fact that the 'old Frey' and I seem to have been quite alike works well for me. That's not to say I'll take this second life for granted,*" Frey pondered. "*Both Alva and Carolia appear to have accepted that I won't 'recover' my memories. That's probably for the better, all things considered.*"

Alva peeked out over the branch again. She noticed him in deep thought with eyes fixed on something far away. "Frey?" she asked. There was no response. "Freyyy?" Still no reaction. She took a deep breath. "FREY!"

Startled, Frey nearly jumped out of his hole. "What, what?! What is it?!" he exclaimed frantically as he looked around.

"Calm down. It's nothing," she said with a soft voice and a sorry look on her face, regretful to have spooked him. "I just wanted to ask if you wanted to go home yet. You didn't answer. What were you thinking about?"

"Oh… No, nothing important. Just daydreaming a bit," Frey answered with a faint smile. "*Yeah, it'd be better for us all if no one knew about me.*"

For a brief moment, Frey intended to get up and head back to the orphanage. A gentle wind swept through the forest and caressed his cheeks. The dirt under him had warmed up some, and he could not hold back a yawn.

"*It's not so bad being a kid again—if you can even call what we had a childhood. No duties day in and day out, no daily meetings, and no tiresome sword and archery practice. And of course, no diplomatic relation maintenance or those damned high society parties. No, none of that here. Just peace and tranquility. This feels like... absolute heaven,*" he thought and shut his eyes to enjoy the blissful freedom.

"Hey, Frey-," Alva said and sat up. She stopped when she noticed his closed eyes and slow breathing. Before he took the chance to tell her he was ready to go, he fell asleep. "Oh, well. It's not a big deal. I guess I could let him sleep for a while before we go home. Maybe I should do the same?" she whispered and shuffled back in her spot.

Several hours later, the sky turned a vivid orange as the sun wandered closer to the horizon. Alva was the first to wake up and did so with a mighty yawn. She looked over to Frey, who still remained soundly asleep.

"Frey..." she muttered as she rubbed her sleepy eyes. Frey did not react. She got up and went over to him with sluggish steps over the uneven ground. She crouched down and gently shook him by the shoulder. Frey slowly opened his eyes, and for a few seconds, he looked around, confused, until his mind caught up to him.

"Well," Frey stretched his arms up. "What do you say? Should we head back now? I think this was a nice 'short' break," he joked.

"I think so," Alva replied, amused. "Granny must be wondering what's taking us so long," she said and offered him a hand up. He grabbed it, and she pulled him up on his feet. Then he froze.

"*This feeling... Are we being watched? Is someone spying on us?*"

Frey looked around, wide awake and on alert. If there was someone there, they concealed themselves well. Though he saw none in the area, he felt their stare on him, ready to kill; it was a feeling he was all too familiar with.

Alva noticed his odd behaviour and looked around herself. "Is something wrong?"

The unsettling feeling Frey had disappeared, and he felt they were alone again. "*Maybe I'm mistaken. I just woke up after all, and my mind's been playing tricks on me ever since I ended up here,*" he reasoned in silence. "No, it's fine," he told her, his voice unnaturally stiff. If it was only his imagination, then he did not want to worry her for nothing.

Alva was not entirely convinced, and although she was a little suspicious, she decided not to press the matter further—worried that it might upset him.

"All right then. Come, let's go home! I'm getting kinda hungry," she announced with joy as she pranced down the path home with Frey close behind her.

They had barely left the tree behind them when Frey found himself fixated on Alva's empty hands. It took him some time before he remembered.

"Ah, damn it!" Frey exclaimed, annoyed.

"What?" Alva stopped.

"The basket—we forgot it back by the tree! I'll run back and get it. Do you want to come with me?" Frey asked and turned around, ready to leave.

"Do you remember where it is?" she asked. Frey nodded in response. "Then I think you'll be faster on your own. I'll be right here but hurry! I'm starving!" Alva complained.

Frey set off up the sloped forest and disregarded caution. As he approached the tree, he went to where Alva sat just a couple of minutes ago. There he found the basket on the ground, untouched. When he kneeled to pick it up, the feeling of being watched came back. Again, there was nothing to be seen. The feeling disappeared as quickly as it came. Then he heard it—the distant scream pierced his ears: Alva's. Frey's heart sank, and he set off like a bolt through the forest.

"I knew it. I knew something was wrong! Why, why did I ignore it?" Frey thought, furious with himself. *"If she's hurt in any way, it's on my hands. My instinct never deceived me before, and I still ignored it! Damn it. Damn it! I can only hope now."*

As he followed the same path he had now taken twice, Frey soon reached the point where they had last seen each other. Alva was nowhere.

"Alva!" Frey called. He shouted her name several times with no response.

A heavy, eerie feeling thickened the air; it was as if the very forest itself held its breath in anticipation. Frey noticed a trail of broken branches and trampled shrubs down the side of the path; it was a new route leading deeper into the forest, seemingly created by something large.

"She must have taken off through here and chased by whatever made her flee," Frey deduced as he flew straight after them without hesitation. The uneven terrain made quick movement difficult, even though most of the path had already been flattened.

Frey reached a small clearing. Clear indentations in the overturned soil hinted that something heavy had run past. Some of the nearby tree roots and trunks had deep carvings, the latter also with large dark patches around the cuts.

"Burn marks?" Frey briefly thought. It was all he had time to notice before he heard Alva scream for help. He turned his head to the direction of it and barely spotted where their trail continued. *"That was close, very close!"* His heart raced as he sprinted through the forest, feeling faster than ever. Nimbly, he ducked and weaved under low hanging branches, his feet barely touched the ground.

All Frey's fears came true when he reached an open glade. From atop a tiny ridge leading down to a sunken clearing, he saw Alva backed up against a tree. With her face full of dread and arms and legs covered in bloody cuts, three large, grey-furred bodies cautiously approached her with hungry eyes. Larger than any other creature of their woods, they growled loud and deep.

"These are… feral wolves? In our forest? What the hell are they doing here?!" Frey thought and slammed his fist against the tree he hid behind. One of the wolves' ears twitched and turned its head, though it warily kept an eye on Alva. *"Have I become too complacent here, too carefree? Was I lazy? Yes. I can't blame this on anyone but myself. Damn it all! Am I forbidden a quiet life, even here?! Just for once! This, all this will have to wait. I must correct my mistake before it's too late."* A voice spoke; it was his own.

"That doesn't matter. I'd never leave you!"

Those were not words that he had ever spoken or thought of, but it mattered not – they drew out the strength he needed to save Alva, no matter the cost.

Frey used the opportunity of the one wolf's distraction and picked up a hefty rock. He had a clear shot from where he stood. When it turned its head back to Alva, he chucked it with all his might. The rock hit its mark and struck the side of the wolf's skull; it cried out and alerted the other two of Frey's presence. Even though one of them had been hit, they were reluctant to take their eyes off Alva. It bought Frey a tiny bit of time. During those precious few seconds, Frey closed his eyes. He focused and laid one hand flat against the tree. The magic was all around him and became more apparent the longer he tried to sense his soul. Weak at first, it was there; it flowed around his body with the wind. It ran like electricity beneath the bark. His senses sharpened as he continued to attune himself to Setura's ambiance – a process that made him feel as if time passed slower. Gentle warmth gathered under his palm, and he lifted his hand off the tree. A single leaf slowly fell as he watched the faint heat blaze up into a ball of fire. With no time to think, Frey braced himself, moved out of cover, and hurled the ball at the wolf that he struck with the stone. The impact sent the beast flying straight into a tree. Its fur lit up as if it had been soaked in petrol, and it could do little more than howl in agony as it writhed like a worm on the ground.

Frey exhaled sharply, relieved. *"It worked... It worked! My magic, I still have it!"* he thought, overjoyed.

The wolves turned around, and their glares invoked the same feeling he had earlier.

"So, it was them after all. They were the ones stalking us. They're massive; how could I not have noticed them before?" Frey thought and readied himself for battle. Unexpectedly, they ran off into the woods. Although surprised, he wasted no time. He leapt off the small ridge and reached her in a matter of seconds. "Alva, Alva! Are you okay?!" he shouted.

"No-no-no, not-again-not-again!" Alva rambled endlessly with vacant eyes, completely oblivious to Frey's presence.

" *'Not again'?"* Frey wondered, though he knew now was not the time for questions. He crouched down and quickly checked her body for any signs of serious injuries, ignoring any smaller cuts. She was fine as far as he could tell. "Alva!" he said with one hand on her cheek and stared directly into her eyes.

Alva went silent, and her eyes moved. She looked back at him and slowly recognised him. "F-Frey?" she whispered. "Frey? Frey! What are you doing here?! W-we have to run. There, there are *things* here! We have to go, now!" she shouted in panic.

"Calm down. Just breathe, okay? Everything is fine.

We'll be fine," Frey told her in a calm but assertive tone.

"Fine?! No, we have to run. Now!" she yelled, beyond terrified. She tried to grab hold of him to run away, but Frey resisted.

"Alva, I know. I saw them. Look," Frey told her and pointed to the wolf on the ground. Its fur was burnt away, and its exposed flesh was charred. *"Strange… The fireball was nothing special but caused such damage. Are the feral wolves that weak? Maybe it's got something to do with Setura,"* he noted.

Alva stared at it in disbelief. "I-it's dead…? B-b-but how? Was it-, was that you?" she stuttered, overwhelmed by the sight of its remains.

"It was. Do you believe me now? We'll be fine."

"No way. No way. There's no way you did that. You can't have!" Alva dismissed and proceeded to laugh nervously. Frey looked at her with steady eyes. Then she grabbed him by the shoulders. "What do you mean it was you?!" she shouted and shook him wildly.

"She's in shock. This is pointless," Frey thought with a tired smile. He gently grabbed her hands and took them off him. "Listen to me, Alva. Take deep breaths and try calming down. We're not safe yet. They're still here."

The bushes rustled as the feral wolves ran around them. Frey could hear their heavy panting and the sound of their paws hit the ground.

"What do you think I'm saying?! Please, let's get away while we can! Let the mage deal with them!" Alva pleaded.

"Mage?" Frey repeated, surprised. The wolves went silent. Suspicious of them, Frey stood up to face the remaining predators. Alva grabbed the back of his shirt to pull herself up but faltered and grimaced in pain. Frey caught her before she fell. *"Ah, I see. That's why the chase ended here. She must've sprained her ankle,"* he concluded and carefully let her down.

"You're hurt. Please don't try to move, or you might make it worse. This will be over soon. I promise." His voice was calm, assuring. However, it only confused Alva further.

"W-what are you saying. What do you mean?"

Frey sighed. "Even if we got away, the feral wolves would remain here – alive. What if their next targets are unable to defend themselves, unable to run? They would probably die, and it'd be my fault."

"What are you talking about? How would it be *your* fault?! The mage should deal with them—not us! Please, let's get away from here!" Alva shouted in desperation on the verge of tears.

"Take a look around us," Frey told her and straightened up. "There's no one else here but you and me."

Puzzled, Alva stared at him. She glanced over to where the fireball came from, subconsciously having remembered its path. When she saw no mage there, she also noticed the lack of any other sound. There were no spells cast nor the voice or figure of anyone else nearby.

"There's no one here," Frey stated and faced the centre of the clearing.

"What? What are you doing? Don't, please…" Alva mumbled, terrified, as she grasped for his shirt again. In sheer panic, her eyes searched for the non-existent mage when she jumped to the sound of flames blazing right next to her. A bright fire burned in his hand; he looked right back at her with glee. *"N-no way. It-, it was Frey?"*

"Do you see now? There's nothing to worry about," Frey assured her with the warmest smile.

"That fireball…it killed the wolf in one hit," Alva thought, eyes fixated on its burnt corpse. *"Frey did that, but how?"*

Frey spotted blurry shadows sprinting amidst the trees. The sound of their deep breathing was louder than before.

Agitated by the fire, he expected them to strike at any moment.

"Alva, I need you to listen to what I say. Can you do that?" he asked without turning around.

"I– I can," she confirmed, though with a complete lack of confidence.

Frey could only hope. "This is important. Look at me," Frey said and turned his head slightly. Their eyes met. Alva had mostly returned to normal but was still very much afraid. "Remember, breathe and stay calm. I'll make sure you're safe. Stay alert, and don't take your back off that tree for a second, got it?"

Alva nodded in response. Frey stepped forward toward the middle of the glade, and Alva shuffled backward, anxiously keeping an eye on the edge of the clearing.

"They should be tempted to attack now that I'm out in the open. I killed one of them easily, but that's no reason to lower my guard. If anything, they might be more dangerous. They're here, waiting. I can feel them staring, wanting to rip me to pieces." Frey patiently waited for them to make their move.

The panting stopped. Then the bushes exploded when a feral wolf lunged at Frey in a silver-grey blur. Frey remained still. The wolf leapt through the air and came to an abrupt stop when it slammed headfirst into an invisible wall; it shimmered upon contact and then faded away. Stunned, the wolf stumbled around to regain its footing.

Frey shook his head, dissatisfied. *"Weak. How disappointing... The barrier wasn't even concealed, yet it couldn't even detect its presence. Ah, I know it wouldn't be anything like duelling a mage's familiar, but I thought they'd put up a little bit more of a challenge. They're quite intelligent, there's no question about that, but in the end, they're just animals. Honestly, I don't get the fuzz over feral wolves."* He sent a wave of fire with a swift motion of his right hand that engulfed it and turned it to ash scattered by the soft wind.

The third feral wolf burst out of the shrubbery on his left with its eyes set on Alva. Frey reacted and turned to it. He lifted his hand as if to say 'rise.' Enchanted golden chains erupted from the ground. Ensnared, the wolf howled and snarled; it used all its might to break free but to no avail.

With two wolves down and the third one securely restrained, Frey noticed his heavy breathing. "*What's this feeling? Did I use too much mana?*" he worried. He threw another fireball that whizzed just past the chained wolf. "*No, that's not it. Maybe my body just is not used to magic? Maybe. That can be remedied through training. But then, to what extent can I use it? If I can cast a more powerful spell, I know I'll be fine. I should try, but first...*"

Frey set aside his concerns and hurried over to Alva.

"Are you okay? Can you move?" he asked and kneeled beside her.

"My foot... it hurts pretty bad. I can't stand on it," Alva told him, careful not to let him touch. She looked up to him with wide-open eyes. "What was that, Frey? How can you use magic? Why didn't you tell me anything?" she asked, amazed and hurt that he kept something that important from her.

Frey was silent. Should he tell her the truth: where he was from, who he really was– or should he not?

"*...What do I even say? I can't just go: 'Hey, so I'm not actually Frey! I'm someone completely different. Oh, and by the way, I'm not even from Setura!' No, that's absurd. Who would even believe it?*" Frey debated with himself; his own feelings remained unclear. Impatient as he was – a trait he had gained in Setura – he decided to postpone their discussion. "I know you have questions. I'll try to answer as many of them as I can, but first, there is something I have to do. If all goes well, I'll be done here. Then we can talk for as long as we need to." The way he spoke was friendly but also incredibly persuasive.

"Promise you'll tell me everything," Alva requested. Frey found it difficult to refuse when she looked at him with pleading eyes.

Frey hesitated. *"Everything? Ah, whatever, we'll deal with it later."* He nodded. "I will. Everything. Now, let's get you somewhere safer."

Alva reached up and wrapped her hands behind his neck when Frey went to pick her up. Albeit a little uncomfortable, she was not wholly opposed to it. She even noticed her heart beat faster in his arms. At the edge of the clearing, there was a tree nearly identical to the one they napped under earlier. On the far side, Frey found a small pocket between two hefty roots—just what he was looking for.

"This is a perfect spot. You'll be safe here," Frey said as he lowered her down.

"Safe from what?" Alva asked, worried by his choice of words.

"Nothing – I hope. But it's better to be safe than sorry, right?" Frey told her. Though he appeared confident to Alva, a small part of him was not as sure. *"Magic is mine to command. It* will *obey me as it has before,"* he told himself.

Frey approached the wolf with determined steps. Exhausted, it remained suspended in the air; it was held perfectly in place by the chains. Even while subdued, it was evident that a feral wolf was a ferocious hunter, worthy of respect. Its intensely yellow eyes observed Frey, just as much as he did. It cast an eye towards Alva, who stuck her head out from behind the tree.

"Wonder what spell I should use for this test? Maybe I should try Absolute Zero? Katja always used it whenever we got the chance to practice. Hm, no. Ah, I know!"

"Why is it looking at me? Could it-," Alva thought, unnerved.

"Alva! Can you hear me well?" Frey shouted and

interrupted her thought.

"Yeah?" she shouted back.

"If I tell you to take cover, make sure you flatten yourself against the ground as much as you can! You can't hesitate! Do you understand?"

"Got it!" Alva replied with a thumbs up.

Frey took a deep breath and cleared his mind.

"Right, then. Here we go," he said under his breath.

Frey closed his hands together and raised them up as if to catch something that fell from the skies. Warm air gathered around his feet, slowly turning around him. It gained speed and heat; the wind turned chaotic as it clashed against the surrounding cool air. It tugged on his clothes and ruffled his hair. He began to pant.

"This again? I know I have enough mana, or it would've already dispelled itself. I should be careful... but I need to know where my limit is. I already waited too long to test my magic. I can't be unprepared again."

Deeply focused, Frey was unaware that the wolf had taken its eyes off him and Alva. Instead, it glared at something past either of them.

The wind changed and converged into a single point in Frey's hands as one stream. A small vivid orange flame appeared. As it sucked more of the surrounding air to fuel itself, it turned from a warm orange; to hot red; to bright sapphire blue.

"It's so hot. How in the world is the grass not on fire? And Frey stands there as if it was nothing," Alva thought, unable to help herself from catching a glimpse. She was forced to shield her eyes from the excess hot air currents and the bright light. Despite the noise created by the spell, she heard a twig snap behind her. When she turned around, her jaw dropped.

Frey opened his eyes. Time slowed down, and he was

met by a brilliant sight. Luminous strings of magic slowly swirled around the blue flame, consumed by the fiery core. As stunning as it was, a strange, disturbing sensation lurked beneath the beauty of it all – it was an omen. His focus was broken by Alva screaming his name in sheer panic.

From the shadows, a fourth feral wolf flew out from behind them—its fur a deep, dark blue shade.

Frey threw out his hand toward her. One of the chains that held the trapped wolf in place let go and flew at it in blinding speed. It wrapped itself around the dark wolf's body right before it sunk its teeth in Alva. Frey grabbed the chain and pulled it back. The wolf was sent flying in an arch trajectory and slammed into the ground next to the chained wolf, where it left behind a prominent dent. The chain wrapped itself around its front and hind legs, so it could no longer pose any threat.

Frey's broken focus resulted in the flame core becoming unstable. It fiercely refuted his control and freely sucked in the surrounding air to grow brighter and hotter. Whips of fire lashed out from the core; each strike ignited leaves and grass. The wild magic applied a tremendous force on his body, a feeling much like what one would experience if standing underneath a cascading waterfall.

"*This won't work. I can't stop the airflow,*" Frey thought, barely able to remain on his feet. "Alva, get down now! Whatever you do, don't look up!" he yelled to her at the top of his lungs.

Terrified, Alva was stunned for just a moment before her body obeyed her mind, and she crawled down into the pocket and pressed herself against the dirt. She shut her eyes tightly and braced herself for the worst.

Frey turned to see if Alva was at least out of sight. Satisfied, he directed all his attention to the flame. He could only hope there were no more hidden surprises. The searing heat originating from the flame even affected Frey, a consequence of the uncontrolled magic, and he struggled to endure it much longer.

"*If I don't dispel it soon, a first-degree burn will be the least of my worries. Not only will the whole forest burn down, but Alva probably won't make it either…*" Frey thought, sweat dripping down his face.

Frey tried to close off the flame's air supply by creating a magic barrier around it, but it proved to be an impossible task – much like trying to close the door of a flooding room.

"*It's no use. I can't dispel it. It's going to blow! I need to try and redirect the blast away from us; it's our only chance,*" Frey asserted. He drew upon every bit of his remaining strength in an attempt to fling up to the sky. However, the core flame had been out of control for too long and turned volatile. As soon as he tried to move it, it released its stored energy all at once in an ear-deafening blast.

Frey opened his eyes with a high-pitched ringing in his ears as the world spun wildly around him. He was on the ground with his back against a broken boulder. Smoke filled his lungs and burned his throat whenever he breathed in. All the trees around him were seared black, many of which were broken in half. The two feral wolves had been reduced to smouldering piles of flesh. Frey could not keep his eyes open any longer.

The silence which followed was ear-deafening. Petrified, Alva expected Frey to call her name at any moment. After what felt like an eternity, Alva started to move in her hiding spot. Slowly she raised her head to look around. She sat up and covered her mouth, using her dress as she coughed uncontrollably. Her sooty body ached terribly from the blast's shockwave. She looked up to see that even the mighty oak tree she used as shelter had its upper half blown away.

"Frey!" Alva screamed in terror when she saw him

motionless on the ground. Her voice caused his closed eyes to twitch.

Alva pulled herself together and stumbled across the uneven ground. She gritted her teeth from the sharp pain that came with each step on her foot. Nearly there, she tripped and fell to the ground. Determined to get to him, she crawled the rest of the way.

"Frey! Say something!" Alva yelled frantically and gripped his arm.

Frey opened his eyes and was met by Alva's fountain eyes and trembling lips.

"Frey!" she exclaimed in relief and pushed herself off the ground to embrace him. "I thought I lost you," she mumbled with her face buried in his shirt.

Frey tried to suppress the pain that came with every breath. "Hey, there's no need to cry. We survived," he told her with a hoarse voice and forced smile. "I can barely believe it; we survived. Are you hurt, Alva?"

"A little, but you look like you're in a lot of pain," she answered and looked up, worried beyond belief.

"Oh, no. I'm just fine," Frey said, somehow able to manage a bit of sarcasm. "*If I didn't put the barrier up in time, that blast surely would've been the end of me, but… it was incomplete. Who knows how it managed to absorb enough of the explosion?*" With death successfully averted, Frey raised his weak arm and reached out to Alva. "Grab my hand." Alva listened and put her hand in his. Frey tried to focus, a challenge as good as any with his dizziness and injured body.

The ground beneath them gave off a verdant light, and with it appeared strange green particles that gently floated upwards. A soothing warmth enveloped them; little by little the pain subsided. The ringing in Frey's ears faded away, and the aching in Alva's foot and body disappeared. She sighed with relief.

Frey gasped. *"Finally, I can breathe properly. Pretty sure more than half the bones in my body were broken. That's what it felt like anyway. Thankfully, I still had mana to cast Revitalise. I don't think I would've been able to make it back,"* he thought facetiously, aware he would have gone nowhere. "Can you walk?"

"Maybe. My ankle doesn't hurt anymore," she thought and placed some weight on it. "Amazing..."

"Would you give me a hand then?" Frey said and reached out to her with a smile, drained and exhausted. Alva grabbed it and pulled him up.

The duo took a good look around the devastation. Frey remembered his promise. While not wanting to go back on his word, he worried any guards from the village would show up and see him.

"If you're all right, then we should get away from here," Frey said, grabbing her hand and running before Alva could object.

The pair ran and ran. The more distance they gained the greener the area became until they finally reached the edge of the forest. Frey remained standing after he caught his breath while Alva sat down by a naturally fallen log.

"Why did we have to run?" Alva asked, still breathing heavily.

Frey did not answer. Instead, he stared down at his shaking hands. Furious and frustrated, and against his better judgement, he shouted and threw wave after wave of scorching fire in the air. Then, he slammed his burning fist into a rock, crushing it with ease. The fire was extinguished. After a few seconds, he turned around and sat down next to a shocked Alva. Magic aside, she could not recall ever seeing him this emotional before.

"God, I'm such an idiot! A failure as a man, a mage,

and, above all, a friend! Something wasn't right. It wasn't! Any fool could have seen that! How the hell could I allow this to happen?!" Frey thought, so ashamed and angry with himself he nearly burst into tears, unsure what else to do.

Unexpectedly, Alva took his hand, placed it in hers, and leaned her head on his shoulder. She sat completely silent for a few minutes while Frey calmed down.

"Thank you…" Frey eventually managed to say, his voice uncharacteristically shaky and uncertain. A little time was all he wanted, needed.

Alva lifted her head and saw his bitter look. "Frey, what was that?"

He did not answer; instead, he squeezed her hand to try and stop the trembling.

"Frey… if it's about earlier, it's fine. I won't make you tell me anything. You—I don't think you would keep secrets from me for no reason." She spoke with a soft voice, drained of all her energy like him. "You saved my life. I thought…I really thought that was the end for us. Thanks to you, I'm still here, alive."

Frey began to turn, to look at her, but then stopped and instead rested his head against hers. The last thing he wanted to do was to hurt her more than he already had done.

"If you truly want to, I'll tell you everything, everything I know. But if I do, most of it won't make any sense, and I think a lot of it will hurt. I really, really don't want to do that to you."

Alva knew that whatever it was, it weighed heavy on his shoulders. "I want to know; I won't pretend I don't. Being kept in the dark is not a fun feeling, you know?" Alva took a deep breath as she made up her mind on the matter. "I won't force you to tell me—for now. But you'll have to promise me that you will if I ask you again one day."

"I promise," Frey said with eyes locked on the rolling

plains far away. "If you still want to know then – whether it be tomorrow, in ten years, or a hundred – I'll keep nothing away from you. I promise you."

"You better not forget this too…" she mumbled.

"*Too*?" Frey repeated. Alva pretended not to have heard him. Frey sat up and looked up at the darkening sky. "There is one thing I can share with you, though, if you want to hear it," he told her to get their mind on something else. "You can't tell anyone about it though, not even Carolia! Could you do that?"

"'Course, I can! I won't tell a soul!" Alva answered earnestly and straightened up. "It's not something bad, is it?"

Frey smiled at the thought. He took a moment to gather his thoughts. "No, no. It's not. I'm sure you are aware of this already, but I'm no stranger to magic. In fact, I'd like to believe I know it quite well. Whenever I concentrate on it, I can feel it flow all around us – like water in a calm river. Usually, it's nice and serene."

"Really, is that what using magic is like? Do you think I'll get to experience it too?" Alva asked, keen to learn more.

"When you first learn to use it, almost certainly! But as you get used to it, you probably won't notice it as much."

"Oh… Is it that way for everyone?" Alva asked, disappointed.

"I think so," Frey replied. "*At least when it comes to normal magic.*"

"That kinda sucks," she pouted. "Um, so… What happened back there? Do you know? If you can't tell me, that's fine, but it was terrifying. I thought we were done for."

Frey shook his head. "I don't know. Something felt off when I fought off the feral wolves. For some reason, it felt like using magic sapped away my stamina. That's part of the reason why I wanted you to move somewhere safer. In hindsight, I'm glad we did."

"Does that mean you saved my life twice then?" Alva

asked and managed to make him smile a little.

"Maybe," Frey answered, appreciative of her effort. "You wouldn't have been in that danger, to begin with, had I not decided to test that spell. Maybe I'm the one who risked your life?"

"Hm, I don't think so. Did you know what could have happened?"

"I was ready for something. I…" Frey had to stop and cleared his throat. "I never would've expected it to end up like that though. Now I know that there is something *seriously* wrong with me," Frey told her and looked down at the ground. He pulled up his legs and leaned forward with crossed arms, his confidence shattered. "*As for what, I don't have the slightest idea.*"

"You shouldn't blame yourself for not predicting the future. If you hadn't been careful, I probably wouldn't still be here. But you were! You did what you could," Alva told him to try and cheer up his gloomy self. Unfortunately, she reinforced his idea that he was to blame for everything.

"*I didn't. None of this would have ever happened if I didn't ignore my instinct in the first place. I can't afford another mistake again; I definitely won't allow it. There might not be a 'next time.'*" A minute later, tired of his own thoughts, Frey stretched out his legs and let out a sigh of resignation. "All right, all right. I hear you. Thank you, Alva. I appreciate it," he told her with a warm smile. Alva was happy to see Frey feeling better.

"Sooo, now that you can use magic, what are you gonna do?" Alva asked with a hopeful look on her face. "...Will you come with me and the Oracle?"

Frey held off his answer. A part of him wanted to stay with her—to see her grow. That very feeling also made him uneasy at the thought of being apart. At the same time, something whispered to him that his future – along with the answer to what happened to him – lay elsewhere. Where, though, he had no idea.

"I'm sorry. I won't," Frey told her with a heavy heart.

"I see…" Alva failed to hide her disappointment. "Why not?"

"To be perfectly honest, I don't think there is much more to learn from studying at a school. I would much rather travel around Vallendar—maybe even in the neighbouring countries. I want to explore more of Setura and especially learn about how people use magic! I don't think being a student will allow me that," Frey explained.

"Oh, but I thought you were already a magic expert?" Alva teased him.

Frey chuckled. "There are always things to learn, *especially* when it comes to magic! But I'm not convinced what I seek lies within academia. It's out there, somewhere, and I know I'll find it eventually!" he told her; his passion to explore the unknown shined through.

Alva knew it was pointless to try to convince him otherwise. "If that's what you want to do, then I'm pretty sure there's nothing I can say."

"I'll be looking forward to seeing you again after you leave. You'll have to show me how much you've grown as a mage," Frey told her with a warm smile on his lips. The way he spoke was affectionate and familiar.

In contrast to Alva, Frey, curiously enough, had no real concerns about being away from each other. It wasn't because he did not care for her—he had grown to do so greatly. Rather, it was because he was confident that she would grow and thrive on her own. As a friend, Frey felt heavily indebted to the kindness Alva showed him and the help he received over the past two weeks. He considered going with her to repay his debt that way, but he could not deny the overwhelming desire to travel down his own path; Alva knew this well.

"Geez, I haven't even packed my things yet," Alva said when she was reminded of it. "I'm sure it'll be a while until I can even cast a spell or fight like you can."

"Don't be so certain! Some people learn and improve faster than others. It's no different when it comes to magic. If the Oracle said you have a lot of potential, then I can only assume you have a great talent. Take your studies seriously, give it your all, and you'll surprise even yourself!" Frey encouraged her, confident in her abilities.

"You really think so?"

"I *know* so!"

Alva smirked. "Do you think I'll be stronger than you then?"

"Who knows?" Frey shrugged. "We'll have to see, won't we?"

For some reason, his playful answer made her laugh, which rubbed off on Frey. Maybe they laughed out of relief because they finally felt safe? What was certain was that Alva had come to accept that there would be some things about Frey she was unaware of, though she found comfort in knowing that all she needed to do was ask. Meanwhile, Frey was glad to know what he told her was enough and that she respected his wish to travel. Their eyes wandered to the open plains in full view from where they sat. Stars emerged to dot the deep blue twilight sky.

"It feels unreal to sit here and laugh after all that's happened today. That's a strange feeling after everything I've been through. I wonder what she's thinking? I guess it doesn't matter. She's a strong girl; that much is obvious. She'll be fine. Our paths will cross again one day. I know it." Frey admired her strength in silence.

"Can I ask you something else?" Alva interrupted his thoughts.

"Of course."

"What was that spell you used, the very last one? It felt like my skin was gonna melt off. I couldn't breathe. It was scary in a way, even before... you know, *that* happened," Alva said in a mixture of fascination and fear.

"Ah, that one? It's a spell called Nova. It gathers all the air in the area into a single point to fuel a small flame. The flame heats up and grows in power over time before it unleashes the stored energy in one burst," Frey explained, much like a teacher.

"It sounds like it's powerful. Is it hard to learn?" Alva asked in awe. Each question revealed more and more how interested in magic she was.

"Mastering it is difficult, but the reward is great. It's hard to evade once cast, and defending against it is next to impossible. I don't know of any protection spells that work against it. With that said, it's also extremely dangerous. As you've seen first-hand, if you ever lose focus while channeling you may end up paying for it with your life," he told her in a serious tone. Magic was not a force to ever underestimate, a fact best to be remembered.

Alva grumbled. "That's weird, though... Is the spell in Setian? It doesn't sound like the Lost Language."

"I know Setian is the language spoken in Setura, but what is this 'Lost Language'?" he thought, puzzled by her question. "What do you mean?"

"The, um, Lost Language?" Alva asked. Frey nodded. "I don't exactly know. I got to talk to the Oracle when she came to visit us last year. I had some questions for her. Mostly, I was curious about what they could teach me, and she told me that before anything else, I would learn something called the Lost Language."

"And that is?"

"I think it's used to cast spells. Because it's 'lost,' there is little we know about it. Apparently, every cast was a guess at first. Although it's rare to come across unknown spells nowadays, it still happens. But Nova sounds like Setian to me," Alva said with furrowed brows.

"Another language is used to cast spells in Setura? Good thing I found that out now. I'll have to be careful in the future," Frey thought. "Alva, please make sure you don't mention this to anyone else either. Okay?"

"Sure, I won't. I don't get why you're being so secretive about everything though. First the magic, now this Nova spell," she told him, confused by the reason behind it all.

"I—I just want to live my life in peace. No one can bother me if there's no one around to know, right?"

"Are you embarrassed about where you come from...? The village, I mean," Alva asked, disheartened.

"You're joking. Where did you even get that idea from? Not a chance!" Frey laughed. "If you're asking if I'm ashamed coming from 'just another poor village,' then you couldn't be more wrong! This place, this village is richer in so many other ways!" The tight-knit community that made up Delera village left a lasting impression. People worked tirelessly to make sure everyone in the village at least had food and shelter, even at their own expense.

In his past life, Frey spent a good portion of his spare time in the countryside; life in Setura brought him back to then. On top of that, the love and care their caretaker showered them with reminded him of some of his childhood. His parents rarely had time to spend with their children, so naturally, he grew close to the man who helped raise them. It was him Frey thought of whenever he saw Carolia. Despite not being their mother, she treated them as her own—especially Alva.

"I'm happy you feel that way, Frey," Alva chirped. "I agree: there is no place better than home! Well then," she exclaimed and hopped up on her feet, "I think it's time we go back. I'm sure that even the dragons heard that explosion. We really shouldn't worry Granny anymore."

"You're right," Frey acknowledged and pushed himself up.

"And don't you worry; your secrets are safe with me!" Alva told him with a cheerful, radiant smile.

Alva and Frey reached the outskirts of the village just as the last of the sun's rays faded away in the night sky. Delera was lit up more than usual; its residents indoors, and the guards stationed outside wore full armour and with hands ready on the swords hanging on their hips. The two returning children were spotted by a pair of soldiers who went to meet them.

"Hey, you!" one of them shouted as they approached. "Where are you coming from?"

"From the forest!" Frey answered with deep breaths in feigned panic.

"The forest you said?! Are you injured? Do you know what happened?" they asked.

"I-it was feral wolves! It would've been the end of us if that mage didn't show up to save us!" Frey told him with a trembling voice. "But something must've happened. When he told us to run, there was this huge explosion!"

"What? A feral wolf attack – here?" the second guard asked. "That explosion must have been the sound we heard. Is the mage okay? Do you know? What did he look like?"

"I-I don't know. I didn't see his face. I don't know what happened. Everything just went dark… When we woke up, the forest was on fire. I couldn't see him anywhere. We just—we ran as quickly as we could…" Frey told them in a flawless performance of deception in hopes of not being asked too many questions. It worked.

"I think that's enough. These kids have gone through enough for one night. We'll leave it for another day," the first guard interjected. "You guys have done well. Go on. Go home and try not to worry. We'll make sure the village stays safe!" he said and placed his heavy hand on Frey's shoulder.

"Thank you, sir…" Frey said in a low voice. He grabbed Alva's hand and ran to the orphanage. He glanced back and saw the guards return to the others.

"*I would've been found out instantly. Where did he learn to lie like this?*" Alva thought.

The two reached the orphanage where they saw Carolia at the door, speaking with the village chief, an elderly man.

"Granny!" Alva shouted and ran ahead.

"Alva, Frey! Thank the heavens you're safe!" Carolia explained and embraced Alva.

When Frey witnessed her relief, he could not help but feel a little warmer on the inside. The bond between the girl and her grandmother was as strong as mother and child. He felt excluded, but since he thought of himself as an outsider, it did not bother him.

"The guards said something serious happened in the forest! Since you hadn't come back yet, I went out looking for you. I would've still been out there if the guards didn't make me come back. Oh, I was so worried," Carolia told them, beside herself with joy.

"*She really went out on her own to find us?*" Frey thought, surprised. "We're fine. You don't have to worry anymore," he said to try and calm her.

"I can see that," Carolia sniffled and wiped her tears using the apron. She opened the door. "Come in, children. Come in."

"I'm glad everything turned out well, Miss Carolia," the village chief said after Alva and Frey had left. "Didn't I tell you there was never anything to worry about?" he leaned in and whispered with a gleam in his eye.

"I know, Rolan. I just can't help it. You know what she

means to me," Carolia told him.

Rolan chuckled and turned around, ready to leave. "Have some faith, Miss Carolia! It's all we've got left!" he encouraged her. "But I hear you. I'll speak to Edriel and see what he has to say for himself. I should be back before the girl leaves. Please let our village know I'll be away for a few days," he said as he left down the road with slow steps and glanced back at her. "…You look tired, Miss Carolia. Make sure you get some rest while I'm gone!" He waved and disappeared into the night.

"Thank you. I will," Carolia smiled back. She went inside to the kitchen where Alva and Frey sat by the table, exhausted. "Would you like some tundra berry leaf tea, my dears?"

Alva and Frey nodded in response, too tired to speak. Carolia grabbed a kettle from a cupboard, filled it with water, and placed it on the burning hot stove. She dug out a wooden container and three hand-carved cups from the back of a shelf and put them on the table. The nearly empty container held dried white-red leaves.

Alva laid her head down on the cool tabletop with her arms stretched out, and Frey leaned back on the bench.

"Today might just have been the worst day of her life or at least one of the worst. She was hunted down by feral wolves, almost died, and still pulled through! I would've loved to watch another mage grow, but I've already made my choice," Frey thought as he observed her. He already began to miss her.

After no more than a few minutes, a loud whistling sound came from the stove. Carolia lifted the piping hot kettle off the stove and moved it to the table. She poured the hot water into each cup; within seconds, the brittle leaves in the cups melted away and dyed the water red. It gave off a fresh and sweet fragrance.

"What happened there, children?" Carolia asked and sat

down on a chair between the two. "We heard an explosion; all the guards were put on alert immediately."

Alva sat up and looked to Frey, uncomfortable and lost as if to ask him what to say. Frey noticed her look but did not meet her eyes.

"It was crazy. We just woke up from a nap and were on our way back when I realised that we forgot the basket. I ran back to get it but," Frey paused. He quickly glanced at Alva before he continued. "Alva got attacked by feral wolves and-."

Carolia's wrinkly eyes opened wide in horror. "You were what?!" she blurted out and cut off Frey.

"I'm fine! I'm fine, Granny. I hurt my foot and had some smaller cuts, but I was healed. I don't think I've ever been that scared though…" Alva told her, still gravely disturbed whenever she thought back to the feral wolves.

"You- you were healed? By who?" Carolia asked.

"When I finally caught up to her," Frey continued, "there was a mage who fought them off. The wolves backed off after he killed one, so he healed Alva while I kept an eye out."

Carolia remained silent for a few seconds and eyed them both. She exhaled loudly. "My word, I can't believe a mage happened to be nearby. What about the explosion?"

Frey shook his head. "We don't know. We were about to run when we were suddenly knocked away. I must've passed out because when I opened my eyes again, the mage was already gone along with the wolves. Alva picked me up, and we ran—ran as fast as we could." Frey was convincing in the way he spoke. He was confident in his story, yet there was a taste of fear in his words.

Carolia sank her head into her hands. "If only I hadn't sent you there. This is all my fault," Carolia mumbled, weighed down by guilt.

"It's not your fault, Granny. How could you possibly

have known they were there?" Alva told her and grabbed her hand.

"She's right," Frey chimed in. "And besides, we're alive and well, right?"

A tear of joy formed in the old lady's eye. "Come here, you," she said and pulled them in for a hug. When she let go, she gently placed her hands on the side of their faces and looked them in the eyes. "I hope I can thank that mage one day. He doesn't know how much you mean to me."

Alva sat down with a yawn. "I'm so tired I feel like I could sleep for years," she stated and stretched her arms up.

"It's no wonder, dear. You should head to bed before you close your eyes one too many times. I wouldn't want to ask Frey to carry you to your bed!" Carolia teased.

Alva shot out of her seat all flustered. "I'll go. I'll go! Geez, what's with everyone making fun of me today?" she mumbled bitterly as she left for the bedroom with sleepy eyes and rose-red cheeks.

Frey smiled. *"Could you be any more obvious? Not that it's her fault after a day like this. Who would have the energy to keep up appearances in her shoes?"* Amused by the thought, Frey gazed out the window to the night sky with his hand wrapped around the hot cup. The two moons were obscured by the smoke that blew in from the forest.

"Shouldn't you go to sleep too, Frey? I'm sure you must be tired," Carolia asked after a short while.

"Probably," Frey replied and took a sip of his tea—his eyes locked on clouds floating away in the distance. For the first time in what felt like forever, there was nothing on his mind. He could sit down in peace and enjoy the warmth spreading through his body. Once done, he stood up and covered his mouth in a yawn. He left the table, but upon reaching the door, he stopped and turned around.

"I'm sorry we worried you," Frey told her.

"You don't have to apologise. You're home and safe. That's all that matters," Carolia told him with a wrinkly, old smile.

"Good night," Frey said, happy she was at ease.

"Good night, Frey."

When Frey entered their bedroom, he saw Alva already buried under the many covers of her bed. He went to his bed next to Alva's and laid down with his face against the pillow. He breathed out; the fatigue he had been ignoring hit him all at once as the tension in his body was finally released.

"Maybe this was more stressful than I allowed myself to think?" Frey thought. He got up and turned around to lay on his back. "Night, Alva."

"Night, Frey," Alva's muffled voice replied.

Frey looked up at the ceiling for a bit before he closed his eyes. There was the sound of rustling armor in the distance. His breaths slowed down, and the beat of his heart grew louder as everything else faded away.

***

Frey opened his eyes. Surrounded by impermeable darkness, the only thing visible was a faint, strange light far away.

"What's this? Where am I?"

Frey looked around slowly as if submerged in dense liquid. No sound came out of his mouth when he tried to speak. Faint screams and suppressed rumbling resonated from afar. His eyes searched for light; it was now much brighter and closer than before. He began to suffocate.

"I-I can't breathe..."

Paralysing dread took hold of his body when he saw what the light truly was – a colossal, fiery meteor aimed toward him. It stained the nothingness with an eerie red shade and grew brighter until he had to close his eyes and look away.

He saw and heard nothing but felt something pull his clothes.

As the light faded away, Frey opened his eyes. He found himself somewhere he had never been before, atop a hill, surrounded by countless corpses in a wide-open area. The ground was shattered and in flames. He wanted to get away; several ruined buildings appeared when he turned around. The main structure had a magnificent clock tower, and some of the other buildings were covered in massive cracks while others were partially collapsed. The clock tower remained standing, though entire chunks of it were missing. When Frey took a closer look at it, he saw the clock's arms spin backward. The buildings disappeared, replaced by silhouettes of people far away. Something within drove him toward the figures. They turned around to face him when he got closer. He thought he saw them wave and shout something to him but heard nothing.

"What's going on. What is this place? Who are they? What happened here?"

He was overcome by weakness and fell to his hands and knees where he came face to face with an endless abyss visible through cracks in the ground. The silhouettes dissolved into nothingness, and the fissures widened before his very eyes as the ground opened; it swallowed the bodies, buildings, even the ruined earth itself until it was all gone. Again, he was surrounded by naught but darkness. A deep fear washed over him, and the deafening silence caused sharp pain in his ears. Though the terror soon passed, the feeling of powerlessness remained. He regained his strength a little at a time until he could finally stand up, though with some difficulty from the disorienting void. When he looked up, he saw the human silhouettes again. He approached them and was able to make out four different figures. Three of them were together: on the far left, a small person with waist-long flowing hair; in the middle, a slim, well-built man with long hair; to the right of him, another woman with equally long hair, neatly tied up. On the far right of them all, a third woman stood all alone, separated from the rest. The man went closer to her and reached out his hand; only then did she join the others. They all appeared to be young adults except for the smallest person who resembled more closely a child. Frey stumbled toward them. Something called out to him. However, the closer he got, the slower he moved. Suddenly, something pierced through the small girl's body – Frey froze as if he had been turned into stone. The other two women flinched, and the young man's silhouette began to shake and thrash wildly before he yelled something from the depths of his soul. Frey could not look away or close his eyes. Something disturbing stirred deep within him that made him sick.

"What am I seeing? Who are they? What's happening to me?"

"You…" a young woman's voice said. A pale face with thin, bleak lips appeared. Everything else was obscured by long hair. The silhouettes behind it disappeared. "You… You," it mumbled with a heavy rattling breath.

"Me?"

"You… You. It's all your fault! You!" it screeched in harrowing fury.

Frey jumped out of his bed, his heart beat wildly, and his sheets soaked in sweat. Frantically, his eyes searched the room only barely lit up by Luna's weakened light.

"It-it-it was just a dream?" Frey thought and swallowed hard. He glanced over to Alva still in her bed as he caught his breath. *"More like another nightmare…"* He reached for the half-empty potion flask and took a sip of it before he placed it back on the bedside table. He laid back down and closed his eyes.

Chapter 3.

"The Oracle"

Lyra 1 416

Three days had passed since the feral wolf incident; it was the day Alva turned fourteen. Frey had come to learn that birthdays were mostly celebrated by the wealthy. For commoners, someone's birthday was little more than another day of the week. However, this day was special for an entirely different reason as Delera village expected the Oracle's return.

Frey and Carolia sat down by the kitchen table, each with a cup of cold, icy blue Winterleaf tea in hand. Alva stepped through the door in very different clothes. Gone were her ragged garments. Instead, she wore a loosely fit, verdant green dress with long sleeves and a short skirt and a pair of black heeled boots. The dress and boots were handmade by the village's tailor and leatherworker. Though simplistic in design, the comfort and high quality made them all the more charming.

"Those are your new clothes? You look great! They really suit you," Frey told her, impressed by craftsmanship.

Though excited and nervous for today, Alva was happy to hear Frey's compliment.

"Have you finished packing?" he asked and took a sip of his tea.

"I think so. It's not like I have a lot to bring with me anyway," Alva replied and made her way over to the table. She sat down next to Frey and leaned her head on him, which shook the cup in his hand. "What about you? You're also leaving today, right?"

"Yep. I finished packing yesterday, though," Frey said and nodded at an old leather bag by the door.

"It looks a little empty. Are you sure you've got all you

need?" Alva asked as if she were his mother instead of his friend.

"As you just said: it's not like I have a lot to take with me," he replied jokingly. "A change of clothes, some food, and bandages if needed. Just the essentials." His new clothes were donated by the tailor the night before.

"I know. I know. Why'd you want to go to Siria anyway?" Alva inquired, a little curious of his destination. It was a choice made with Carolia's help.

"The capital is the centre of Vallendar. All sorts of people walk in and out the city gates day and night. There should be plenty of places to stay and rest—and work to do! I think it's the best place to start," Frey explained, looking forward to his trip.

"You've really thought this through, huh?" Alva said and leaned back on the bench, secretly hoping that a certain someone would be able to persuade him.

"Siria is also not too far away from here. It's what, three days distance by foot? Doesn't sound too bad to me!" Frey added.

"But shouldn't you come with us then? I think the Oracle lives in Siria. I'm sure they wouldn't mind you accompanying us there!" Alva suggested, hoping to spend more time with him.

Frey raised his brow. "Does she? If it's true, I don't see why not. I'm not dressed as nicely as you, though. Do you think it matters?"

Alva gently shook her head. "She's not like that," she said, referring to the Oracle. "I don't think she'd mind it at all."

"Frey, what is it that you seek in Siria?" Carolia asked. It was a question that had been on her mind since Frey decided to travel there.

"What I seek?" Frey repeated and put down his cup on the table. "Hm, good question. The knowledge of potion brewing is valuable, but I think what I want the most is to discover what types of magic there are and how it's used. Even if I can't brew anything myself or cast magic, obtaining and understanding that knowledge will certainly be valuable. Whatever happens after that remains to be seen!"

"I must say your aspirations are quite unusual for a boy your age. Despite being unable to use magic, you're still interested in it!" Carolia remarked, proud of his ambition.

"You think so?" Frey said with a smile.

Carolia nodded and smiled approvingly. "With that sharp mind of yours, I'm sure you'll be fine. You better not forget to write me a letter every once in a while, and share what you've been up to! Alva promised me she would."

"Of course, I won't forget," Frey replied, though he was not yet sure how Vallendar's postal service worked, seeing as one apparently existed. "Oh, but I'm sorry we barely got to do any herbalism, Carolia. I do appreciate everything you've taught me so far, though!" Although not much, Frey was taught some of the basics of herbalism. He was also given one of Carolia's books on herbalism which was already packed in his bag.

"Nonsense, child! My only wish has been for the two of you to one day manage on your own. Having watched you grow up into brave, fine young people, it's clear that I have nothing to worry about!" Carolia said with nothing but love. A mischievous smile spread across the woman's old lips. "But I must admit, I thought the two of you would stick together forever," she said and glared at Alva with a smug look on her face.

Alva blushed. "What do you mean by that?!" she blurted out and shot out of her chair, all while Frey calmly sipped on his tea.

"Oh, nothing at all," Carolia replied and waved away Alva's confrontation. Alva sat back down, flustered.

Soon after there was a commotion outside.

"The Oracle! It's the Oracle! She has arrived!" voices shouted, soon drowned out by the sound of hooves and squeaking wheels.

Alva let out a heavy breath. "Well… I guess it's time."

The three stood up and left the kitchen. Alva crouched down to pick up a brand-new knapsack, made of a soft maroon fabric and held together by leather straps, in the hall by the main entrance – another gift given to her by the village tailor and leatherworker.

Frey was the last one to step out of the door. Three large wooden carriages stopped a few paces away, surrounded by a good portion of the village residents. Some of the armoured soldiers and robed mages dismounted from the first and last wall-less carriages to convene with the village guards while the rest secured the immediate area. The door of the middle carriage remained closed. Carved into its azure-coloured walls were beautiful hand-painted flower motifs. The view through its windows was obstructed by white drapes. Each carriage was pulled by two luminous creatures: spirit horses – only similar to their non-spirit counterparts in shape. They were handled by a pair of guards. White-blue in colour and with a pair of radiant eyes, spirit horses were slightly larger, faster, and possessed far greater stamina than any other steed. Certain parts like their slender legs or magnificent manes faded into vague transparency.

Two guards approached the middle carriage and the door opened. A man stepped out, dressed only in a white robe and a red rope tied around his waist. His combed hair was straight and short; its lighter brown shade complemented his chestnut-coloured eyes. A fair-skinned, young girl followed. The man offered a hand to help her down the steps. She wore a pure white, sleeveless dress with the symbol of a dove embroidered on her chest. A veil obscured her face, yet Frey caught the glimpse of a smile.

"That must be the Oracle. As Carolia said, she's young," Frey thought, surprised by her age and height when she approached Alva.

"Welcome back!" Alva cheerfully greeted the Oracle.

"Thank you. I am happy to be back! Delera has a certain calmness about it," the Oracle said with a soft-spoken voice.

Frey kept his distance by Carolia's side to not disturb them in any way.

The village chief appeared down the road. "Welcome back to our humble village, Lady Oracle! I trust your journey was both short and pleasant," Rolan greeted her politely. Despite his old age and scrawny appearance, his mind remained sharp. He knew well the significance in being chosen by an Oracle and gave Alva the entire village's support— perhaps so that one day Delera would stand to gain from her potential.

"Your concern is appreciated, village elder. Thankfully, Delera is not too far away from Siria," the girl replied. She turned to face Alva and continued, "Let us get right to it. Have you decided on what it is you want, Alva?"

"I have," Alva said and gripped the leather straps of her knapsack. "I've decided to come with you," she revealed, nervous but confident in her choice.

"Do you really mean it? Oh, that is wonderful! I am so thrilled to hear it!" the Oracle exclaimed and grabbed Alva's hands in unbridled joy.

The way she suddenly expressed her emotions contrasted sharply against how she spoke or behaved mere seconds ago—at least in Frey's eyes. He was used to people holding important positions or held in high regard to behave in a more reserved manner.

"My Lady, please. Mind your appearance," the white-robed man pleaded – clearly of the same though as the young boy.

"He doesn't look too old. What could he be: twenty, twenty-one? He looks younger than I am," Frey thought and grinned. Now closer, Frey noticed dark circles under the eyes of the robed man. Although tired, he remained courtly and spoke with respect.

"Oh, what is wrong with it, Arner?" the Oracle said and turned to her aide. "Allow me to be happy for once! You know I was certain she would not come with us!" she said and turned back to Alva. "I am so glad. I truly am. In all my years, I have never seen someone with as much potential as you, Alva. Whatever you need, I will do my best to arrange it!"

Arner gave up his efforts and glanced over to Frey and Carolia when he noticed the boy's gleeful smile. Arner remembered him from their last visit, but something was different about Frey though he could not put his finger on what. "My Lady, is that not the boy you spoke with on our last visit?" he whispered to her ear.

"Hum?" the Oracle uttered. She turned silent for a moment when she turned to look at him. "Is it? How strange. I was wondering..." she mumbled before she walked up to him. "You are Frey, correct?"

"That'd be me. Have I done something wrong?" Frey asked, unsure if she noticed his laughter.

The Oracle went in for a close inspection. She mumbled something unintelligible as she paced around him and occasionally poked at him.

"Pardon me, but what are you doing?" Frey asked, feeling like an item being examined.

"Oh, um!" the Oracle exclaimed and jumped in surprise, brought back from whatever deep thoughts she was in. "It is nothing, maybe... You are Frey, right? You sound like him, but something is different. Very different..."

"Of course, I am. Can't you tell just by looking at me?"

Frey asked, unsure why she had to ask.

"Looking? What do you mean?" the Oracle said and lifted her veil. She looked at him with fogged, ice-blue eyes. Her blindness took Frey by surprise. "It is the price all Oracles pay. One sight in return for another," she told him.

"'All?' There are more of you then?" Frey asked.

"Indeed," the Oracle nodded. "We spoke of this during my last visit. I am certain you know this. Or perhaps 'knew'...?" she questioned him. "It may be appropriate if we were to speak in private. Do you mind?"

"Is that so? In fact, I had hoped to speak with you as well," Frey replied, content she was the first to propose a private meeting.

"Excellent. Please, excuse us," the Oracle said to Alva and Arner before she left with Frey to the orphanage.

"As you wish, my Lady. We will await your return," Arner complied and bowed.

Alva was left with a confused look on her face.

Well inside, Frey and Sari made their way to Carolia's private study on his suggestion.

"Please close the door and windows. We would not want to be disturbed," the Oracle requested.

Frey silently complied. Once done, he moved two chairs from Carolia's desk to the middle of the room and helped her sit down.

"Now," the Oracle said, careful not to speak too loudly. "You are not Frey. Who are you?"

Frey was stunned. *"Wait, she knows? How? Then the rumours are true?"* he thought. Initially impressed by her ability, he soon became suspicious of her.

"Please, be at ease," a calm Oracle told him, having noticed his feelings change. "I will not mention this to anyone else."

Sceptical of her intentions, Frey decided to continue

their conversation. "I do not see myself having much of a choice other than to believe you. Yes, you are correct. I am not Frey. How can you tell?" he asked coldly, distrustful of the young girl. The change in his tone was instant. It was dignified and formal, completely unlike how he had been speaking previously. His otherwise friendly and inviting look was replaced by one without emotion and a gaze that could freeze a wild bull in place.

The Oracle took a moment to think of how to best answer him. "Us Oracles, perhaps you already know, have many rumours circulating freely in cities and kingdoms alike. For the longest time, these rumours have led to fear, respect, and a desire for our abilities. One rumour in particular mentions how we can see the souls of the living."

"And you say this rumour is true?"

"While our special sight is considered an invaluable asset, it came with a price. Everything you can see, from the grass waving in the wind to the clouds high in the sky, I cannot," the Oracle told him, careful not to speak with emotion in regards to her duty. "But what I can see is magic in its purest form, and, yes, our souls."

"Hm," Frey grumbled. He appeared rather indifferent to her tale. Then he chuckled as the answer laid bare. "And you are saying that my soul is not the same as when you were last here?"

The Oracle confirmed but added there was a similarity between the two.

"Similar, you say? Well, your ability to distinguish such a thing is nothing short of incredible! It appears this is one secret which cannot be kept from you," Frey remarked. As he was well familiar with the human soul, he now discovered that the Oracle could differentiate one soul from another. He was also aware of the possibility that she could tell whether or not he spoke the truth. "*I wonder if she sees souls the way I used to. She had to give her sight for this ability. Although Varius made sure I suffered no permanent harm, it was not the most pleasant experience when I had to attend to my duties.*"

"Besides, the Frey I met had no aptitude for magic," the Oracle continued. "He would never be able to use it, but you… After a closer look at you, your soul is powerful – exceptionally so."

"I will take that as a compliment," Frey said shamelessly, though the Oracle appeared concerned.

"Something is not right, though," the Oracle said with a frown.

Frey narrowed his eyes, unsure what she meant. "*Not right*? Explain."

"Every person I have met had their souls look similar. They are beautiful, much like a fiery aura that shines in different colours and encompasses their bodies. Although they are so alike, I can tell them apart by their various, minor differences."

The way the Oracle described her special sight was just how Frey remembered it. To see the difference between souls was for her a task no different than telling faces apart. "What makes mine different from anyone else's?" Frey asked to discover any clues which might explain what had happened a few days ago.

"It is strange…" the Oracle told him but then turned quiet. "Apologies, I find it hard to explain. If I put it this way: While everyone else's soul looks like a gentle flame, yours is erratic. It twitches and does not evenly envelop your body as it should. May I borrow your hand?" the Oracle asked and reached her left hand out to him. When Frey placed his hand on hers, she moved her right hand to hover above it. "Move it around but only horizontally. Do you see how my hand follows as you move yours?"

"Yes."

"Do you see how my movement is delayed and a bit off? That is because of your soul. Normally, I would be able to mirror your movement perfectly. Now I am unsure and have to guess." Frey kept moving his hand and watched as she tried to stay as close to it without touching. No matter if he moved it fast or slow, she could never quite line up her hand with his.

"I see what you mean," Frey said and pulled away his hand. *"Something is wrong with my soul? If I can trust her word, then this is far more serious than I could have guessed."*

"I do not know why this is." The Oracle was visibly troubled by the fact that she had no answer as to why his soul behaved the way it did. She continued to speak, "You should be able to cast magic. I know this much. Have you tried to? If you did, did something happen?"

Frey was hesitant to share more than necessary. However, he took into consideration that she already knew what he kept secret ever since his awakening and appeared keen to help him understand himself.

With carefully chosen words, Frey told her what he knew. "There was an accident weeks ago. I was told I was struck by lightning. When I woke up, I had no memories of Setura or my past here. There was also another incident just a few days ago where I had to use magic. Something happened when I tried to use a high-tiered spell and it nearly killed me and Alva," Frey told her, still ashamed by his failure. "Do you think my soul may be the reason why we nearly died?"

"A high-tiered spell?" the Oracle thought, surprised. "If you, for whatever reason, were certain that you should have been capable of such a spell, then I see no other explanation than there being a serious problem with your soul."

"I *know* I should have been able to use it," Frey told her, his voice had not the slightest trace of doubt.

The Oracle shook her head, trying to make sense of what Frey told her. "I have never heard of anything quite like this before – a broken soul. And for it to inhabit the body that once belonged to someone else… This would explain why you can't remember anything from before the lightning strike. I cannot imagine how it must feel," the Oracle stated. She sat up and looked at him with pity. "I presume Alva knows of your ability to use magic. Does she know, well, who you are?"

"No," Frey replied. "We spoke after my disastrous blunder. I told her my feelings on the matter—that now is not the time for her to know. I firmly believe she would suffer far more than she would benefit from knowing," he explained to her.

"I understand. May I ask you, what will you do now? If I am to be honest with you, I would very much like you to come with me. I have never seen something like your soul before. It would seem Delera has no shortage of surprises!" the Oracle laughed before she continued, "Perhaps we could discover the truth of your soul if we work together?"

"Thank you for the offer, Miss Oracle, but I must decline," Frey politely rejected her suggestion. "Alva asked me something similar. With all due respect, I believe I can find out more on my own, unrestricted by anyone or anything. Besides, I have a desire to travel all around Vallendar and in Setura. I am afraid if I come with you that will not be possible."

His rejection came as a surprise. "If that is the case, I cannot hide my disappointment. I will respect your wishes. Both of you have the right to make your own choices. That is the reason I refused to force her to come with us on my last visit—or this time," the Oracle said.

"Now that we have mentioned Alva, I do have two favours to ask of you, Oracle," Frey said and straightened his back.

"How bold of you to request such a thing, especially when this is the first time we meet." She turned stern and appeared insulted by his straightforwardness. When Frey was about to apologise, she suddenly broke out into small laughter and smiled. "That is what I should be saying, but I still cannot get used to behaving that way! Of course, I will gladly hear what you have to say!"

"Oracles seem to have quite a history. The way they're expected to stand, walk, and talk is surely demanding. Even I hated to act this way whenever there were meetings or when mingling with nobles. This girl must be around twelve maybe even thirteen. I'm glad she can remain cheerful, even when carrying such a burden," Frey thought as he reflected upon the girl sitting before him. His eyes lit up when he realised what had vexed him ever since the first time that he heard her speak. "Oracle, before I give you my requests, I have a single question for you. Could it be that the reason you have given Alva such freedom to choose is that you lack your own?" he asked, and her smile vanished.

"You are one to speak of impressive abilities…" she said in a low voice. A few seconds passed before she continued to speak. "I admit, it is as you say. I rarely have the time to do as I please or do what I would otherwise like to. As you might know, one of my duties involves finding young talented mages – like Alva – and bringing them with me to arrange their education. For the rest of my time, I am expected to be always available as the king's advisor, to meditate, and pray. This takes a lot of time and leaves little room for other, less important activities."

Frey watched closely as she spoke. She was much more reserved than before and a bit saddened by his unexpected question.

She recollected herself and continued to speak. "It is a lot of work. Nonetheless, despite my demanding duties, I am alive and healthy. I never need to worry about my safety, nor do I ever need to hunger. It is my privilege to play a vital part in the future of our kingdom, and for this reason, I am grateful.

I truly am."

Though she appeared happy and content with her life, Frey was not easily swayed. *"Hmph. I don't need to see your soul to know that's a self-told lie..."* He leaned over and stared at her with piercing eyes, annoyed by the way she tried to convince him. Though bothered, the reality is that there was little that could be done. He straightened up and continued, "I know you carry a heavy burden on your shoulders. I am certain it would be even heavier for someone your age. You have given up much for what you believe in. Make no mistake: I do not agree with it, but I still admire your strength. If your dedication and will is not already an inspiration to all, then it by all rights should be," Frey told her, hoping she would remember his words if ever needed.

The Oracle knew he saw through her façade – that she did in fact often wish for a simpler life – and let out a deep sigh. "Your perceptiveness is something else, Frey. Yes, as you have discerned, my life is one lived inside a golden cage. Even so, I would never give it up. What I said earlier holds true. I am vital to our kingdom's future and its safety. For this very reason, I refuse to bend or break."

Frey could not help but smile. The determination she possessed was uncommon and strong; he knew it would carry her through hardship. Without thinking, he gently stroked the top of her head, much to her surprise.

"You don't have to tell me that. I know you won't."

As he looked at her, an image flashed before his eyes. Instead of the Oracle, another young girl, a few years older with long, silver hair stood before him. He could not see her face but caught a glimpse of a blissful smile.

"Lynn..." Frey then snapped back to reality and pulled away his hand. He unintentionally treated the Oracle the same way he did his youngest sister. "I-I'm sorry! I didn't mean to do that." He worried his actions would be interpreted in a

demeaning manner.

The Oracle was confused for a moment but soon cheered up. "It… it's fine," she said in a soft voice. She cleared her throat and continued, "It felt calming, reassuring, but you seem troubled. Is something wrong?"

"I-, well…" Frey stuttered and stumbled over his words. He tried again after taking a breath and told her briefly about the 'dream' he had before waking up in Setura. When she asked whether it was a dream of his past life, he could not answer for certain, only that it brought pain. *"These memories… I can't tell if that's all they are. It felt as if I relived that precise moment. It's way too real. Come to think of it, didn't I hear something that one time? It was her voice, wasn't it?"* he pondered and thought back to his first day in Setura. The harder he tried to remember it, the cloudier his memory became. Frustrated, he decided to switch the topic. "Anyway, that is something for another day," he said and forced a smile, more so for himself than anyone else. "There are still these favours I would like to ask of you."

"Ah, yes. It seems we got a little distracted. I am all ears, Frey. What is it you need?" Sari asked.

"Firstly, I must ask you not to tell Alva anything we have or will discuss today. We agreed that I would tell her everything one day if she still wants to know then. This is the promise I gave her," Frey told her and emphasised just how important he thought it was to them both.

"I understand. If this is something you decided on together, then I will take what I know to the grave. Though I must ask, do you believe there will be a time when she is ready to hear the truth?" the Oracle asked, curious about Frey's thoughts on the matter.

"I do not know. That is for her to decide. She knows that if I tell her, it will not be easy to hear. Regardless, she has my word," Frey answered.

"By the time you meet again, I have this feeling that she will have changed significantly…" the Oracle said. "Consider your first favour done. Now, what is your second request?"

Frey looked the Oracle in her misty eyes, who simply sat on the chair and patiently awaited his next request. "Earlier, I told you that I would not come with either you or Alva. I sincerely do not intend to offend, but I do not believe I could learn much more when it comes to magic, no matter where you would take me. What I can learn is the way of life in Setura and how magic is used by its residents. There are many kinds of people I would like to meet and creatures to see," Frey explained. He showed a genuine desire for exploration of his new home.

The Oracle knew well how much he yearned to travel, both from his voice and his soul. Clearly, she was not used to being turned down as most with magical talent could only hope to be discovered by an Oracle. Nevertheless, she had already acknowledged that Frey was no ordinary person.

Frey continued, "The capital, Siria, is my first point of interest. Alva suggested that I come with you there, but that is not my favour. Instead-." Frey paused. He questioned whether his request was even possible for her.

"Go on," the Oracle urged him.

"Rumour has it that you can see the future. If that is the case, would it be too much to ask if you look into mine – right here, right now?" Frey asked. He dared not hope for anything to help resolve his inner turmoil but figured a glimpse into the future could help guide him along the path he had chosen.

"Oh, I see! Yes, we do have the ability to peer into the future of anyone we wish to aid. However," the Oracle said and raised a finger, "you should know that visions are not guaranteed. I can try, but I cannot promise you anything."

"That is fine. An attempt is all I ask, nothing more," Frey assured her.

"Very well. Let us begin," the Oracle said and reached out to him with open palms. Frey placed his hands on top of hers. "Close your eyes and empty your mind. Breathe slowly but steadily. Fluctuation in a soul will interfere with visions, cutting them short," the Oracle instructed.

Frey followed her advice and focused on a single, featureless point in his head. Seconds later, images flashed through their minds.

"I see… a cave. I think it is in the Enn forest." She spoke in a slow and soft voice. "It goes deep. The tunnels are empty and lightless, abandoned for a long time. A shroud lingers on the ground. It grows. I cannot see much. I-." The vision caused her distress. Her hands trembled lightly, and she breathed harder. Then she relaxed, and her breathing returned to normal. "That strange fog vanished. Now, I see a large room. I see coins of gold litter the ground, ocean blue and fire red jewels everywhere, and the remains of people. It looks ancient. Could it be a lost treasury? I see you. But you… ignore it all? Something else caught your attention. You pick up something. A necklace, a medallion? There is something inscribed in it. It says-." She abruptly stopped and lowered her hands. "I am sorry. The vision ends there. I see now more."

"It ended for me as well," Frey said, disturbed by what he had seen.

The Oracle's mouth opened ever so slightly in shock. "One moment. You… saw the vision too?!" she exclaimed, barely able to keep her voice down.

"I did. Is… that not supposed to happen?" Frey asked, unsure and confused by her reaction. "I assumed that is why you had me put my hands in yours."

"That is only to help me connect with a soul – yours in particular– for the vision to be as reliable as possible," the Oracle told him. "I- I have never heard of anyone that is not an Oracle to see their own vision! How in the heavens?" she stuttered in complete disbelief. "I must ask the other Oracles if they know of anything like this at our next meeting!"

"Ah, one second!" Frey added and put an end to her eagerness. "If you do that, could you wait to bring it up and also make sure not to mention my name?"

"I do not think I can hold it off since we convene so rarely. I should seek their advice as soon as possible. However, I will keep your name a secret," she told him.

"Hm. That is not ideal, but... I understand. Thank you. That aside, I do have a question about the vision," Frey continued.

"Is it about that strange mist?" the Oracle asked. The same thing had been on her mind.

"Yes. Then we saw the same thing. Maybe it is just my imagination, but something felt off once it vanished. Have you ever seen such a thing before?" Frey asked, unsure what it could have meant.

"No," the Oracle replied.

Although her visions often required interpretations, Frey's future remained clear even with its anomaly.

"Visions may be fragmental and not always shown in sequential order. They also may appear differently from how they truly happen. You noticed the fragmentation, correct? The way it jumped from one location to another?" she asked him. Frey confirmed with a nod, and she continued, "To make matters even more confusing, sometimes you may see things of the past. In your case, what we saw can likely be presumed to not have happened yet. However, the order of which they happen remains uncertain. Another limitation I have is that I cannot control how much of a vision I see. It varies and can last anywhere from a few seconds to a full minute. Your vision lasted fairly long. Still, it was a new experience for me. I do not know what to think. It makes me feel uneasy..." she said and covered her mouth while she thought of its meaning.

"Did someone interfere with the vision? Is that possible?" Frey asked, intent to know if he could rely on what he had seen or not.

"That is unthinkable!" the Oracle exclaimed. "Visions are intangible and uncontrollable. Where they come from and why only Oracles can see them is debated. I believe these visions are moments of time seen through the eyes of the gods, a gift from them to help us. There is no magic powerful enough to meddle with it." She shuddered, having thought of something. "I have never mentioned this to anyone, but I believe that the visions may even be beyond their control. For someone able to interfere with that… It is a terrifying idea."

"*I may know more about the Servants and their masters – or gods as most think of them – than most mortals. Yet even I know barely anything about them. She questions something I never seriously thought of. What if time is also beyond their control? The more I think about it, the closer they keep inching to us humans…*" Frey looked at the Oracle in wonder, the girl who had just challenged the very core of the gods – their unfathomable power. He laughed.

"What, what is so amusing?" the Oracle asked, afraid he thought of her a fool.

"*By questioning their abilities, you are but a few steps from rejecting their immortality, their superiority, and the very idea that divinity is beyond human reach,*" Frey continued to think, too busy with his inner monologue to answer her. "*Well, they can die – I know that much. But not by the hand of a mortal. Still, to hear her defy the idea of them in this way is refreshing. I would never have thought to find another human that I could see myself in this soon!*" he thought, thrilled to learn more of the way she thought. He could not help but laugh some more. "Apologies! I promise I was not laughing at you! It is just what you said… I have had similar doubts when it comes to gods, but I could not have expected you to suggest so boldly something this daring! It caught me by surprise!"

Embarrassed, her cheeks flushed red and contrasted against her pale skin. She was certain he ridiculed her for her outrageous belief.

"I cannot tell you why," he said and leaned back against his hand with a grin on his face, "but your way of thinking is not as outlandish as you may think. Whether they have any control over time or not is beyond my knowledge. I do believe that it is naïve to blindly assume they are as omnipotent as many believe, but to hear it come from *you*… I am thrilled to see I am not alone in my doubts!" Frey told her and nearly fell out of his chair from excitement.

"Really? What makes you think that?" the Oracle asked. Frey did not respond immediately.

"*I do wonder,*" Frey thought. "Oracle, I ask you to answer this question as sincerely as you can. You do not have to if you feel uncomfortable. In comparison to the other Oracles, do you differ from them in any noticeable way? For example, the way you think or the beliefs you hold," he asked while gesturing his hand as he spoke.

"I have only met them a few times since I was appointed Vallendar's Oracle. We gather once every winter to discuss topics and visions we deem important," she answered.

"*The way she talks and the tasks she is responsible for. You so easily forget that she's just a child,*" Frey briefly noted.

"While I am currently the youngest known Oracle, it seems to me the others revere the gods more highly than I do – old and young alike. While I do not question their superiority to us, I cannot help but feel they are not as powerful as we would like or need them to be," the Oracle told him. Her faith was strong but, ironically, not as blind as others.

"I share your thoughts when it comes to their power. You need not worry about being alone in that matter."

The Oracle was grateful for his support. "Thank you. I

appreciate it. I do not feel like I can discuss these doubts openly with the others. Even though I can see their true colours, something tells me not to trust them…" she said before she heard the words that left her lips. "What am I saying! I cannot disclose something like this with an outsider! Please, Frey, do not let anyone else know what I said!" she pleaded and grabbed hold of his shirt.

"As I suspected. She seems distant from the other Oracles. Her perception and defiance to any predominant ideas might end up with her getting shunned. I know my world had a long period of time where heretics suffered lifelong imprisonment and torture. Oftentimes, fortunately or unfortunately enough, depending on what awaited them, they were punished by death. It must be frightening to have such a keen mind at a young age – not only if you're an Oracle."

Frey's mind wandered to all the progress that could have been made and all the people who suffered, only because they thought differently over centuries for no good reason. He did wonder if he would have thought as he did now or if he would have conformed back then.

"I don't doubt her sincerity. Perhaps I can trust her too? Then again, now might not be the time either," Frey thought and grabbed her hands to lift them off him. *"Huh, why is she trembling like this? It's like she's scared for her life. She said nothing I would think should warrant such dramatic repercussions. Is Setura this far behind…?"* He tried to put her mind at ease. "Of course, you have nothing to worry about. I owe you for your favours, remember? I will not say a word."

Her trembling subsided, and she sighed out of relief. She knew he meant it.

Frey stood up. "I will not ask you why exactly it would have been such a problem. I would offer my help, but I doubt I could be of much use at this time. For now, let us move on. Before we return to the others, may I offer a word of advice?"

"Advice? I suppose there is no harm in that," the Oracle said with feigned indifference, even if she was curious to know.

"Your senses are sharp and, in addition to your abilities as an Oracle, your insight is surprising. That not only makes you an asset but also a potential threat – mainly to those in power," Frey warned her in a serious tone.

"'Those in power?' You cannot possibly refer to His Majesty?" the Oracle asked and had to suppress her voice, astounded by his apparent insinuation.

"That is not who I was thinking of. With that said, I do not know the King. As such, I cannot guess whether he would see you as a threat," Frey replied.

"Who *do* you speak of?"

"The unseen. Those hidden behind the curtains—the faceless actors who pull the strings from the shadows. Should you get rid of the puppet master, a new one will continue where they left off. They are a plague which cannot be cleansed," Frey told her, his thoughts drew him back to his world – his previous life. As he spoke, a sudden wave of heat swept over him – a deep, seething anger. "*Not even by me,*" he whispered through gritted teeth.

"Sorry, I did not hear you. What was that?" the Oracle asked, though she soon questioned whether she should have. The change in Frey's soul was clear, even if broken. A few silent moments passed before it returned to normal.

"Never mind it. Regardless, you must be sure to never risk your safety the way you did earlier. I do not know what it is you fear, but it is a dangerous weakness to expose," Frey warned her. "One day, I might be able to help you, but today is not that day."

"*Help me?*" the Oracle thought. She struggled to understand what Frey meant to help with or the threat he spoke of.

"If you do not know what I mean, then that is just as fine. Although you are an Oracle, you might not be on their radar yet – hopefully," Frey told her with a sense of optimism.

"*Radar?*" she thought, unsure of the meaning of the word Frey inadvertently blurted out.

"In any case, let us return to Alva and the others. Try and remember what we have talked about here. I will do the same. As with Alva, the two of us will also meet again one day. For some reason, I feel like it will be sooner than later," Frey said and reached out his hand to offer her help up on her feet. She grabbed it and stood up. As Frey was about to open the door, the Oracle stopped.

"Oh, it just dawned on me! My name is Sari. I am pleased to meet you, Frey," she said and introduced herself with a summer smile.

"What?" Frey asked and turned around, confused. "*Oh, right. Hah! That's true. She's been here before. Although she 'knew' me, we were still strangers. I suppose we were both caught up in the moment,*" he chuckled. "The pleasure is all my own, Lady Sari."

Frey and Sari stepped out through the orphanage's main door. Arner, Carolia, and Rolan were in the middle of a conversation – it appeared to Frey that Sari's assistant held Carolia in high regard. Erland and Olav, the village's master tailor and leatherworker, had joined in on the discussions.

Erland was a short, elderly man. He dressed in a simple but warm fur-lined coat and baggy pants, all of which were created by himself. A bag of thread and needles, among other utilities, always hung off his shoulder.

Olav, a burly man in his thirties, stood with his arms crossed and a confident smile on his face. He wore a white shirt and dark pants under a leather apron and thick leather gloves on his hands. He had a pair of goggles on his cleanly shaved head and carried a tool belt around his waist. His children, a young daughter and son in his early teens, waited patiently behind him.

Alva had wandered off to help one of the farmers out in the fields. She spotted Frey and Sari exiting and said something to them before she let go of two bags and ran over.

"You're back! How'd it-," Alva asked as she approached, although she came to an abrupt stop, interrupted by Erland, who suddenly appeared in front of her.

"Oh, no-no-no! Alva, dear, I asked you not to get dirty! Why didn't Carolia stop you?" Erland exclaimed. He muttered something about it being an important day as he whipped out a brush and duster out of his bag. He cleaned her clothes and shoes thoroughly from dirt and dust as she made her way over to the group with slow steps.

"That old geezer sure gets a ton of energy whenever something needs cleaning!" Olav laughed. "It's just a little bit of dirt. Where's the harm?"

Frey was caught up by Olav and let out a light laugh. "I have to admit: you guys did an amazing job preparing for today!"

Olav nodded contently. "You got that right, kiddo! As obsessive as he can be, Erland's eye for quality is incredible. I'm honoured to have been given the privilege to work with him on this," he said and looked over to Alva and Erland, who had effectively come to a standstill. "You should have said something if you were planning on leaving too, boy. We've known you since you were about the size of Maya here," he said and patted the girl's head. "These clothes took a lot of time, but we would've gladly prepared something for you too."

"No worries," Frey replied, appreciative of the sentiment. "The ones Erland gave us the other day are more than enough. Thank you, though."

"Where are they, by the way?" he asked as Frey was still dressed in his old garbs.

Frey gestured toward the orphanage. "Inside, for now," he replied.

Alva, finally with her clothes in pristine condition, reached the group. "You're back! How did it go? What were you talking about?" she asked, keen to know.

"I had some questions for him, and he needed some advice," Sari told her.

"Oh, what kind of questions?" Alva asked and subtly glanced at Frey, who gently shook his head. "*Something else I can't know yet, huh… Well, I've already decided to wait – and with so much that I don't know about, does one more thing really matter?*" She shrugged, aware that if she began to doubt herself now it would eventually bring about regret. She had to accept the choice already made and did so happily. "I get it, but you can tell me what advice you wanted, right?"

"Yeah, I just wanted to know if she could look into my future before I left Delera," Frey answered, having omitted the details.

"Wait, really? You can do it just like that?" Alva asked the Oracle. As it was not brought up during her last visit, Alva was surprised to learn Sari required no lengthy preparation. "What did you see then?"

"There is this place in the Enn forest Sari saw. I think it'd be in my interest to go there," Frey said, mindful not to reveal too much in the presence of others. "Unfortunately, that might mean I can't come with you."

Alva had disappointment written all over her face. "Really?"

"That reminds me," the Oracle said and turned to her assistant. "Arner, would you please bring me one of my maps? Type 4: Duchy of Siria."

"As you request, my Lady," Arner said and bowed before he left for their carriage.

"You can read maps?" Frey asked, bewildered as to

how.

Sari smiled. "In a way. Since we are blind, we have maps specially made for us. They are based on regular maps but are made so that text can be read with our fingers, and features like forests or lakes are distinct to touch," she explained to Frey, amazed by their technique.

"Is that so? What a remarkable solution," Frey said, thoroughly impressed by how similar their methods were compared to some of the modern equivalents of his world. "What does the 'type' mean?"

"It is a way to organise maps by their content. The type number defines how detailed a map is; a lower number is less detailed but covers more of the world. Whereas a higher number focuses more on a specific region. Ah, thank you, Arner!" the Oracle said when the man returned with a rolled-up scroll. She opened it; her hands ran across the map's surface to determine its orientation. After a few seconds, she showed it to Frey. "Here, do you see this large forest southeast of Siria? It lies between the capital and Delera."

"I see. That's the Enn forest?" Frey asked and pointed at a large green spot.

"Correct," the Oracle replied. "Arner, do you have my pen?"

"I-, you do not have it, my Lady?" Arner asked, confused.

Sari paused, perplexed by his question. "Where would I have it? I have no pockets, no sleeves."

Arner sighed; his annoyance to dig out yet another item was well hidden from everyone but Frey's perception and Sari's sight. With no objection, he left to fetch her pen. Amused, Frey cracked a smile. Once Arner had found and delivered her the pen, she scribbled something on the map.

"It is not too far away from here. Roughly halfway between here and Siria. It, unfortunately, is located in a fairly remote part of the Enn forest. I am sorry, but it deviates too far east from our route," she explained to the disappointment of Alva. "I would say it will take you a day and a half of walking to reach it. It covers a wide area, so I have marked down the general area of where it should be. This is one of my maps, but I want you to have it to hopefully save you some time."

"Thank you. I appreciate your help," Frey said and took the map and rolled it back up.

"If there is nothing else, I believe it is time," the Oracle said and turned to Alva. "Are you ready?"

"As ready as I can be," Alva replied. "Let me go get my bag," she said, passing Carolia and Rolan and everyone else. She went to the orphanage to get the bag on the ground by the door. While she tried her best to keep a brave face, Frey knew by her less energetic behaviour and her mellow voice that it was a difficult moment.

"You are certain you will not come with us, Frey?" Sari quickly asked while Alva was away.

"I am. I know what I want to do, and I want to be free," Frey replied confidently.

Arner wanted to ask why Frey had been invited to join them but refrained. He knew Frey was unable to use magic, which left him wondering what other reason there could be for him to come with them.

"Very well. I expect a letter from you soon – unless we meet again first! Most major cities allow you to post mail. Address it to me, and I will get it eventually," Sari mentioned, intent to maintain their friendship. Alva returned with the bag on her shoulder.

"I'm ready," Alva said.

"Please, allow me," Arner offered to bring her bag onto the carriage. Alva handed it over to him. He climbed up the steps and placed the bag on a fur-clad seat before he stepped back down to wait by the door.

Sari stepped up to Frey. "I am glad we had the chance to speak again, though I am sad to part ways so soon. I hope we meet again soon." She respectfully bowed her head to Arner's horror.

"The feeling is mutual. Until next time, Sari," Frey replied and returned the respect. Sari walked over to the carriage. There, she waited with Arner for Alva to bid her farewell. Alva stood silently; her eyes stared down at the ground while she fiddled with her hands.

Frey knew this was the last time they would see each other for what could be a very long time. He remained silent. Then he approached her and wrapped his arms around her. Alva overcame her nerves and returned his hug with streams of tears that ran down her face.

"You don't have to cry. This isn't the end, you know?" Frey told her in a gentle voice. Alva tried her best not to bawl her eyes out in front of everyone. Frey let go, grabbed her by the hands, and looked her in the eyes. "We both have our own roads to walk down. It might look like they are heading away from each other, but don't be fooled. I can see them cross further down the line – I know they will. Do you?"

"...I do. I do see it. I'm going to miss you, Frey... A lot," Alva said with a broken voice. Villagers who were standing by came closer.

"I'll miss you too. You've helped me more than you might think."

Alva let go of his hands and took a step back. One by one, they stepped up, the old and the young, every person who watched her grow up in Delera or grew up together with her. Everyone wished her a safe journey and success. Many embraced her, and she wholeheartedly returned it.

"Take care, will you?" Alva said to Frey before she turned to the village. "All of you."

The village all replied in a heartfelt response.

"I will," Frey replied. "You better take care of yourself and do your best! I won't forgive you if you slack off!" he said to her jokingly, though he hoped she took his words to heart.

The bond they had developed over the past weeks had grown strong. Inseparable, even before the feral wolf attack, there were few times where one was without the other. To go from that to suddenly living life on their own would certainly not be easy.

"Neither distance nor time will pull you apart," Sari said, about to weep at any moment due to her emotional sensitivity.

"The Oracle is right. You have been together ever since you were small children. You'll be fine, my dears!" Carolia chimed in. She walked up and embraced them both for what felt like an eternity. "I will miss having you around. It just won't be the same. I hope you'll enjoy your new life, Alva. You be good, okay?"

"Don't worry, Granny. I'll make it. I promise," Alva said, her chin resting on Carolia's shoulder. Pearly tears rolled down the old woman's face. Eventually, Carolia let go.

Alva walked up to the carriage. She stopped with one foot on the first step. After a few seconds, she climbed up and sat down on the bench opposite her bag.

"Well then, this is it. Take care, all of you," Sari said and waved.

"Likewise, young one. She is in your care now," Rolan firmly yet politely reminded her.

"Of course," Sari replied. She cautioned Frey to be careful before stepping into the carriage with some help from Arner. She sat down next to Alva and opposite of Arner's seat.

Their escort then climbed onto the wagons, ready to leave. With the crack of a whip, the wooden wheels turned; the carriages kicked up a cloud of dust as they took off.

Alva moved the curtains aside and stuck her head out to see Carolia, Frey, Rolan as well as the entire village wave goodbye; she waved back. They shrunk in the distance with each passing second until they could not be seen. Delera had all but gotten out of her view when Alva sat down with a heavy heart.

"My Lady, why did you bow to the boy? What did you speak about?" Arner finally asked a minute after they had left.

"That is something that will remain between us. It is not of significance anyway," Sari told him, unwilling to divulge their conversation.

"Not significant? How can you say that? You-," Sari silenced him with a raised hand. She felt Alva's sorrow and faced her.

"How are you feeling, Alva? Do you need something to drink?" Sari asked.

"No, no, I'm fine. I'm just a little lonely. That's all," Alva confessed, her eyes avoided them both.

"I know it must be difficult to leave loved ones behind, but do not forget why you did it," Sari told her.

Alva looked up from the floor. Sari said something that made her remember that time she and Frey talked under the tree in the forest.

"Stay strong and faithful to your decision, and you will persevere," Sari encouraged her. It helped, but something else was on Alva's mind.

"Can I ask you something?" Alva asked the Oracle.

"Of course, anything you would like!"

"I was just wondering… Can spells be invoked in Setian?"

***

The dust cloud settled as the sound of hooves faded away. Frey remained still on the same spot where Alva last saw him. By then, the carriages had gone out of sight.

"How odd. The village feels much emptier now. Am I lonely? Did I get too attached?" Frey thought and looked around. Though the village had only lost one of its residents, it felt desolate as some of the village residents had returned to continue their work. "It's strangely quiet, isn't it, Carolia?" he asked after a minute.

"It is," the old woman replied. She took a deep breath and exhaled. "To think, my little girl now has a bright future ahead of her. That's all I ever wanted for the two of you," she said with joy and sorrow on her face. "You're leaving soon too, aren't you?"

Frey nodded, his eyes still fixed on the road. "I planned to go as soon as Alva had left with them. I'll get my bag," he said and headed back inside the orphanage with the Oracle's map in hand. Rolan, Erland, and Olav, in addition to some other villagers, remained outside and discussed the Oracle's rather brief but important visit.

In the kitchen, he placed the scroll on the counter and picked up his bag from the floor. Carolia entered as he went through a final check.

"Frey, do you have a moment before you leave?" Carolia asked, her hands locked together. There was something she needed to know.

"Sure, what is it?" Frey asked as he continued to rummage around in his bag.

"Please, have a seat," Carolia said to him and sat down by the table. Frey stopped, and he looked up. Frey placed his bag by the kitchen table and sat down.

"What's wrong?" Frey asked. He figured it might be something related to Alva. "If you're worried about her, I understand. But she'll be fine – I know it."

"It's about what happened three days ago," Carolia fixed her eyes on him.

"What about it?"

"I want to know what happened that day. What *really* happened," Carolia said. The revelation took Frey by surprise. "You know that Alva's a terrible liar. When she looked at you to make sure she didn't slip up; I knew."

"She knew all this time?" Frey thought, stunned by how Carolia had hidden her knowledge without him suspecting a thing. *"I-. I should have known. She's no fool. Anything less than a perfect lie never had a chance. That's..."* Frey thought before he laughed, much to Carolia's confusion.

"Am I wrong?" she asked, unsure if there had been a misunderstanding.

"No, not at all! That day I thought everything had been covered. I was so certain we could pass this off with none the wiser. Maybe it was because I was so exhausted, but I completely forgot how poor a liar Alva is! In the end, she just couldn't do it. It's adorable!" Frey told her, endeared by his friend's innocence. *"I'm not used to people like her. It's not that they didn't exist. There was just not much room for that kind of a gentle heart. Well, except for* her." Frey thought back to his previous life but only for a moment. Frey acknowledged his failure. "My apologies for deceiving you, Carolia. As I'm sure you know, it was all my idea."

"I'm not demanding you to explain yourself, but I would certainly like to know what happened," Carolia said with saddened eyes, though she did well to hide how much her heart ached.

"I'm still convinced that the fewer who knows what happened, the better for all of us. But she already knew we hid something. Perhaps it's too cruel not to tell her?" Frey debated. He thought about why Carolia allowed them to continue their lie without a question when she had read Alva like an open book. Ultimately, he felt indebted to her—the woman who selflessly had helped him recover so soon and taught him herbalism. *"This can hardly be considered a*

repayment since I kept her in the dark to begin with. Still, it's the least I can do," Frey thought and met her eyes. He agreed to tell her what transpired in the forest on the same condition he gave Alva and the Oracle.

"You have nothing to fear, Frey," Carolia told him with sincerity. She worried what could warrant such seriousness from him.

Frey was happy to hear her promise, knowing he'd be troubled if he were to keep it from her much longer. He retold her what happened, from when they had found the final ingredient, to their rest under the great oak tree.

Carolia's eyes grew fearful when she was told of his intuition and Alva's scream. The boy paused to ensure the glass windows and the door were all shut properly. When he proceeded and revealed who saved Alva and how it happened, her wrinkly old eyes widened ever so slightly, though she patiently remained silent, even when he summoned a flame in his hand. She listened closely as Frey told her of the fight with the wolves and the sudden ambush which led to the disaster – especially to the magic he used.

There were a few moments of silence where Carolia massaged her templates to process everything. When she asked how this was possible, Frey held off his answer. Then Carolia's face turned grim, and she asked: how much did he know?

Frey admitted to an extensive knowledge of magic but would not explain as to how this was possible – now was not the time.

Carolia eyed him in silence. After a few seconds, she let her shoulders drop and exhaled. "I suppose we'll leave it at that." The tired old lady's eyes lit up, and she chuckled. "Well, if that impatient girl can wait, then so can I! Oh, but there is something I don't understand. If you have the ability and talent, why didn't you go with Alva and the Oracle?"

Frey sighed and lowered his head, a little annoyed but

not so much by her. He straightened up. "They both asked me to come. But what I want is to travel and experience Setura! School, no matter in what form, wouldn't allow me to do that."

Carolia asked whether he brought his own desires up with the Oracle, certain that some sort of agreement could have been arranged with his abilities in mind.

Frey had considered it, though he was still not convinced it would have been the right choice for him. "Even if we did, I'm sure I'd still need to dedicate a decent amount of time with them and also deal with certain responsibilities as a student. No, that would only annoy me. I think this is for the best," Frey told her.

Carolia looked at him in admiration and curiosity. "Well, it's clear to me that you have put a lot of thought into this, Frey. I still can hardly believe how you managed to use such powerful magic, but I accept it," Carolia said. Her faith in him remained strong. Something still bothered her. "I'm a little worried that you might end up in a similar situation again. I don't want you to go risk your life every time you use magic. Will you be safe?"

"I knew the spell would be demanding. Yes, it nearly ended us then and there, but it also revealed that something is wrong with me. I spoke with the Oracle about this. Unfortunately, she couldn't help much," Frey told Carolia, though he failed to alleviate her concern.

"That doesn't sound like-," Carolia said, worried beyond belief.

"Simpler and weaker spells than that one should work fine. They should be more than enough to deal with the likes of feral wolves." He was aware of Carolia's feelings on the matter. A combination of the gentle, caring look on his face and the confidence in his voice managed to put her at ease.

Carolia smiled. "All right then. If you're not concerned, then neither am I. That's all I need to know," she told him contentedly.

"I'm glad you asked!" Frey said and lightly laughed.

Carolia raised her brow, unsure of what he meant.

"I wouldn't want you to go around wondering why we lied since you knew there was something we kept from you," he stated.

A peculiar calmness surrounded them as they sat by the table. Carolia was at ease. She knew Alva would be safe wherever the Oracle would take her and now knew that Frey would be capable on his own. Previously, she worried when he decided on travelling through the Enn Forest alone.

"Is it time?" Carolia asked.

"I think so. I've got everything I need and the food you prepared. There's nothing left but to say goodbye," Frey replied and placed the bag on his shoulder. They stood up together, and Carolia followed him outside. The Oracle's map remained on the table.

Rolan and the others stood outside the orphanage. They knew of Frey's departure and waited there to see him off.

"So, the time has come, young boy?" Rolan asked when he came out with Carolia.

"Yep," Frey replied. "I'll surely miss this place."

"And we will miss you. I still remember so clearly when the two of you ran around and caused all sorts of commotion! You grew up to be a fine young couple. Goodbye, Frey. Please do return soon," he said and placed his arm on Frey's shoulder. Rolan was not one to show his feelings, but this day proved an exception.

"Thank you, Elder. I won't forget this," Frey said politely, appreciative of his sentiment. He turned to Carolia. *"Who knows what could have happened if I ended up somewhere else, somewhere not as kind,"* he thought and grabbed his right arm. His wounds had fully healed, but the scars that donned his chest, shoulders, and most of his arm were all but subtle. *"There is no guarantee I would've been able to use magic when I woke up. It's frightening to think that I might've not only be alone but also completely defenceless. I really should have tried using it sooner."*

"Well then, Frey. It's time for us to say goodbye," Carolia said with a shaky voice, saddened to lose another one of her own.

"I won't forget all you've done for me here, Carolia. I owe you for this," Frey said, determined to someday pay her back.

"Please! What else would I have done? Of course, we would help you. Don't you ever think otherwise!" Carolia laughed.

Frey shook his head. "No. The kindness you, Alva, and Delera have shown me carries far more weight than you know. I will make sure to thank you properly one day, all of you," he vowed and looked at Erland, Olav, and the others. "Only time will tell when that is, but I will."

Carolia felt the sincerity in his voice. "If that's what you want, I'll be here waiting. Oh, you have grown so much since-," Carolia said before she stopped herself, worried it might be taken the wrong way.

"Since the accident? From everything you've told me, I can only imagine," Frey replied cheerfully. He was determined to honour the previous owner of his new body.

"I am so proud of you. I really am," Carolia said, barely able to push back her tears. She could not help but hug him one last time. Frey returned it wholeheartedly. With nothing more that needed to be said, Frey turned and walked down the same path Alva had left through. He looked back and waved. Carolia and Rolan did the same.

"That boy is something else," Carolia said to herself as Frey disappeared in the distance. The rest of the villagers left; the sun was still high in the sky and much work remained to be done.

"Does he know?" Rolan asked.

"I don't think so. If he does, it was of her own will," Carolia replied. "What did Edriel have to say?"

"Nothing about the girl," Rolan answered, greatly annoyed by the mysterious person. He glanced at Carolia with a spark in his eyes. "However, he did mention your daughter."

Carolia stared at him incredulously. "Erin…?" she mumbled. There was only one reason why Erin was mentioned – she was still alive. Rolan replied with a slow nod, and Carolia went back inside to the orphanage. Alone in her study and with windows closed, she pulled out a key from under the dress which hung around her neck to unlock a drawer in her desk. Inside laid two dusty masks, one cream-coloured on top of another dark one. She picked up the cream mask and tenderly brushed away the dust; it glimmered faintly.

Chapter 4.

"The Envisioned Cave"

Lyra 4 416

Three days had passed since Frey left Delera village. By now, he could have already arrived at the capital of Vallendar, but he had not even reached the halfway point. For the entirety of his first day, he had done nothing except walk. Well-travelled roads and the occasional sign made navigation fairly simple. Once the Enn forest came into view, he rummaged around in his bag for the Oracle's map. Unfortunately, he discovered that he had forgotten it. Rather than return to Delera, he decided to systematically search the forest using a normal map he brought with him and mark off areas he had already cleared.

"What a stupid mistake. Am I an idiot? If I don't find it today, I'll just have to go back," Frey thought to himself, sitting upon a tree branch with his back against the trunk, greatly annoyed by his blunder.

A lot of time had been spent in search of the cave he and the Oracle saw. Although food and water were of no concern as freshwater streams were plentiful and fish readily available in a nearby small lake, he would much rather have been in Siria by now. The faint sound of voices came from between the trees. As he was in a remote part of the forest, Frey looked around to see if there was anyone nearby. He believed himself to be alone, but something felt off.

"That's… weird. Did I imagine it? It sounded close. Hm, must have been the wind."

Frey called out into the forest to see if anyone would respond, but all that could be heard was the song of nature.

"I don't think there's anyone here. It must have been my imagination," he said and leaned back against the tree after having confirmed nothing was out of the ordinary.

"*Together...*" the faint voice of a young woman whispered in his ear. A chill ran down Frey's spine; he jumped up with a racing heart and searched for the voice's owner behind him.

"*That... was not my imagination,*" Frey thought and held his breath while he intensively surveyed the area around him with fire blazing in his palms, ready to fend off any potential foe.

"*We wanted... Together...*" the voice said again.

This time it was distinct enough for Frey to know who it was. His stomach dropped, and his muscles tensed up; he could not believe it to be true.

"L-Lynnea?" Frey stuttered, eyes dotting around.

There was no mistake; his sister had called out to him. He leapt off the branch and called out her name repeatedly without a response. A bizarre feeling swept in through the forest like the moments before the feral wolf attack in Delera as if the very forest itself had been hexed by something most sinister. The sounds of nature died out in an instant, and the forest's critters had gone into hiding. Compelled by a strange pull, Frey delved deeper into the forest.

"*It can't be. It cannot be. Is she here in Setura? If Lynnea, what about Catherine? I-, I have to find them!*" Frey thought as he hurried through the forest, guided by the unknown.

Soon enough, he reached a secluded area below a smaller, partially collapsed hill. Overgrown shrubbery lined the foot of the cliff. Whatever led him there must have done so on purpose. Frey scouted the immediate area before he investigated the bushes themselves. There, entangled in its many vines, he saw something made of wood. With a swift swing of his hand, a razor-sharp blast of air cut through the bush. The cut revealed a hole in the wall and an old, weathered sign leaned against the cliffside. It carried a warning.

"BEWARE: TURN AWAY"

"This, is this it? Is this what we saw in my vision? If they're here, nothing can stop me from finding them. Nothing," Frey said between his teeth with a fire in his eyes that could not be quenched. His emotions fuelled him. At that moment, he felt he could take on an entire army on his own. Frey conjured a sphere of light in his left hand and placed his right hand on the sign before he dove down into the tunnels. His hand left behind small, golden embers that turned into fire. Within seconds, the sign was reduced to ashes.

Moments after Frey entered the tunnels, he realised the danger of his temper and recalled Sari's warning. Not only could he not be sure where the whispers came from, never mind if they even came from Lynnea in the first place, but he had been uncharacteristically impatient ever since his arrival in Setura. He forced himself to stop and calm down, recognising these caves were an ideal place for an ambush.

"I must stop this childish behaviour. One false step and it could be the end of me. It'd be unforgivable to throw it all away now," Frey thought. He slowed down his breath and took time to focus on the small details on the stone-carved tunnel walls to tame his own emotions. Once he had calmed down enough, he continued with steady steps.

Moisture saturated the air in the tunnels. It made it damp and heavy. Whatever ventilation that may have existed before clearly no longer worked.

"The further down I go, the harder it is to breathe. I'll have to use Breath of Life. A simple spell, not so cheap, though. As long as there are no nasty surprises, I should have plenty of mana to spare," Frey thought.

As he continued his way down, wary of any traps, he noticed a faint shadow-like mist hover above the ground. It always remained just outside the sphere's light but barely visible in the shadows. "*I have a bad feeling about this, but I can't stop now. I need to keep my eyes open and stay attentive. I must continue.*" Frey made his way through the tunnels with careful steps.

After a while, he came across a small room. There was a rotten drawer and a frame hung above it on the wall with its picture ripped out. Two dirty metallic items laid on the ground by the drawer closely resembling rusty candlesticks. Everything inside appeared far more ancient than the sign at the tunnel entrance. On the other side of where he entered, another path continued further and deeper in.

"*What kind of place is this? It doesn't look like the type of place to be used by bandits. These items would be too refined for barbarians like them,*" Frey thought resentfully. He picked up the frame to inspect it closer, and it nearly broke apart from his touch alone. "*I wouldn't want to be caught out here. I should block off the tunnel before I continue,*" he thought and turned to the entrance he came through.

With an open hand toward the tunnel, a freezing cold emerged out of his palm. A wall of ice formed in an instant that extended further than could be seen.

"*Wall of Winter Frost is already tough like steel. It'll be nearly impossible to take down with physical force down here. Its freezing aura makes it resilient versus magic too. This should cover my back well. All right, time to move,*" Frey thought, confident in his magic. He left the room and delved deeper down the rabbit hole.

The roof of the tunnel became lower the further he got, and the pull he felt earlier waned; he questioned whether he went the right way.

"*Was there another path I've missed? No, I don't think so… I still felt it in that room, but now it's almost gone. Should I turn bac– ack!*"

A pulse ran through his body and threw him off balance.

Darkness crept closer as the sphere of light dissolved. The walls spun around him as he desperately reached out for something to lean against, though all he could do was fumble around in the light-depraved underground until he tripped over his feet and fell down to the ground.

"*You said... Together. Forever.*" Lynnea's voice went from a whisper to a heartbroken mumble. Then it screeched, "LIAR!"

The voice echoed in his ears endlessly and blended until only a high-pitched ringing remained. With rapid, uncontrollable breaths, he crawled on the ground until his back hit the stone wall.

"Liar, liar, liar!" the voice repeatedly screamed in anguish.

"I did not– I did not lie… I'm… I'm sorry," Frey mumbled, tears rolled one after the other down his face. "There was nothing I could do! NOTHING!" he screamed in pain and woe.

Frey's voice bounced off the barren and cold stone walls. The chilly stone ground and wall on his back sapped away his body heat while he laid there motionless.

"Liar…" the voice said one final time as it faded away.

Frey remained still on the ground. Every time he blinked, he had no idea whether it was for a fraction of a second or a minute. His tensed-up body eventually gave up, completely exhausted.

Frey shot up and gasped for air, the only sound to break the deathly silence. He cast Breath of Life once more and inhaled sharply a few times before he could start breathing normally. He could only guess how much time had passed while he had been blacked out.

Cold and with a racing heart, Frey created a small fire in his hand to light up his vicinity. Once he had regained his orientation, he placed it down on the ground in front of him where it grew brighter and warmer. Dancing flames cast shadows on the wall behind him; the comforting warmth radiated from it calmed his nerves. He moved up closer to it and stared into the heart of the fire. Its waving light was hypnotising. Frey lifted his hand. It trembled terribly, much like his legs, and there was nothing he could do to help it. He put his hands together and pressed them against his chest.

"Is there a reason why I am haunted so?" Frey thought and stared at the ground with glassy eyes. *"I know. I know! I swore to always protect you. I swore to let nothing tear us apart, but why? Why torment me like this? If only I could turn back time… I-. I never cast you aside. I never once thought of it that way. I love you both. Please, be my strength again. I need you more than ever…"*

A deep emptiness and unbearable sorrow ate him up from the inside. His mind brought him back to his childhood.

"Ever since I took you away from the wretched claws of Mother and Father, I swore on my life to protect you. I didn't. I failed. Maybe I deserve this? Maybe it's my fault after all..?"

Frey's thoughts floated to the final moments before he woke up in Setura—to the one who did the impossible. He saw her in his mind, the one responsible for their death: a royal beauty with eyes as brilliant as her wicked smile. His anguish was quickly drowned out by hatred.

"Isabel… We thought you were our friend. We even allowed you into our family. And you stabbed us in the fucking back! No, this… this is all your fault. Mark my words: If I ever find a way back home, you will pay. You will pay for everything a thousand times over. Even if you hide in death, I will find you. I swear it on my soul."

Frey twitched. *"Did I doze off? It's hard to tell."*

He looked around with squinted eyes. The fire was still there, though it was smaller than before. Unlike earlier, Breath of Life was still active. His body had finally calmed down, and he decided it was time to move forward. With one arm against the wall, he pushed himself up with shaky legs. He summoned another sphere to light up the area, though he could not remember where he came from. The light revealed a grim look on his face.

"*I feel it again, that pull. It's back.*" Though fear had nested itself in his heart, he felt he had no choice but to continue down the path toward the unknown calling's source.

After some time, the roof of the tunnel grew taller. Frey then came across a three-way forked path that all led to a single, large tunnel.

"*Two other paths? Maybe my way was one of multiple possible entrances to this place. My gut is telling me I need to continue straight ahead. Just to be safe...*"

Frey turned around and raised his hand toward the other two entrances, closing his fist. Rows and rows of massive roots broke through the stone to form an impassable barrier.

"*That should be fine. There were no other paths through my tunnel, I think. It'd take quite a while to hack through Nature Barrier's metal roots.*" Satisfied, he continued through the main path.

After a few minutes of walking, the tunnel took a sharp turn which opened into a great chamber.

Frey stayed outside the chamber at its entrance. He grabbed the sphere and tossed it out. The sphere lit up the chamber as if it were day; it turned out to be the very chamber seen in his vision, but to his surprise, there was nothing else they had seen. There was a glaring lack of an abundance of treasure; there was not a single piece of gold, jewellery, or anything of any value whatsoever in sight.

At the centre of the chamber, attached to its high ceiling, was a dusty, spider-infested chandelier with only burnt-out wicks in its sockets. Ruined desks, drawers, and chairs were plentiful. A flight of stairs led up to an elevated floor, which resembled a ruined library with rows of empty shelves.

Frey took one step into the chamber to examine every nook and cranny. Immediately, he leapt back and sought cover behind the corner.

"Something's wrong!"

He cast Magic Barrier, the same unseen spell used against the feral wolves; it was capable against single direct attacks but excelled at protecting versus other magic.

"I felt it, their eyes. Someone's there waiting. I didn't catch who or where they were. **Soul Sight** *will reveal anyone, even if invisible, but can I still use it? After all, it's nothing like regular magic. Whatever, I'll have to try."*

Frey focused and emptied his mind in preparation to draw upon the dormant power hidden beneath his feet, in the air, and behind the walls. He sensed it clearly: a force distinct from Setura's superficial ambiance – ancient and powerful.

"Soul Sight."

Suddenly, the force vanished as if it had simply ceased to exist. Frey tried to summon this power twice more, each time its presence became weaker and weaker. By his fourth attempt, he failed to sense it at all.

"Turns out, no. It must be because of my broken soul. It doesn't matter. I'll have to make do with what I've got. Iron Skin will complement the magic protection. Even if they strike first, it'll give me plenty of time to retaliate."

A silver glow spread from the top of Frey's head down to his feet before it vanished and turned his skin into armour, rendering him invulnerable to any physical strike.

Although as ready as he could be, Frey found himself unable to press forward. Every fibre of his being screamed for him to run away, to not take a single step toward the chamber. Yet the pain in his heart forced him to stay. What if Lynnea was there. Or Catherine? How could he ever look at himself or them in the eyes again if he turned around now, mere steps away from his family? No, walking away was not an option. Frey mustered every ounce of will and pushed himself out of cover.

He had barely taken more than a couple of steps in the chamber before the Magic Barrier shattered like glass, and something hit him in the chest with a thud.

"W-what...?"

He looked down; a metal bolt had easily pierced through his upper body.

"I-impossible. Th-this can't-, this can't be happening..."

Blood seeped through the wound and dyed his shirt dark red as he stumbled forward into the chamber. His hands reached out for something to support himself against, all the while he fought to inhale. Somehow, he had managed to stumble over to one of the tables. His hand went straight through the rotten wood when he leaned down on it, and he fell helplessly to the ground. The bolt's head was serrated; on entry, it had ripped through his flesh and nested itself in his lung and heart. A pool of blood quickly formed under his body.

Villainous, triumphant laughter broke the silence.

"Well, well, well! Isn't this a sight for sore eyes? The great Emperor William the First – assassinated once again!" a warped voice echoed. "Oh, how fortune has blessed me. Though I must say, your current clothing is quite a disgrace for a man of your stature. Just imagine what your people would think! Their beloved emperor, dead, dressed in the clothes of a poor, common peasant!" the voice continued to mock him.

It belonged to a young woman who skipped down the stairs with featherlight steps. She wore black indistinguishable clothing and a pair of simple gauntlets made of hide. Her face remained hidden under a hood.

"*Someone from my world?! H-how the hell did this thing go through...*" Frey thought and reached for the bolt.

Frey's assassin made her way over to him and kicked

him with enough force to send his body flying halfway across the open floor. Blood splattered out of his wound the first and second time his body hit the ground. The woman crouched down by him to take a closer look at his helpless self.

"Don't you worry, William – or whatever it is you go by in this world. The bolt's head is covered in quite a remarkable poison. Not only does it kick in almost instantly, but it also slows down your heart rate. *And* it is one hell of a painkiller! Incredible, isn't it? I wouldn't be surprised if the pain from the crossbow bolt has already faded away! I can imagine how awful it must be to die a slow death. So, I went out of my way to make it as painless as possible. I'm not some kind of monster, unlike you…" Her last remark oozed with contempt.

"W-who, a-are… How…?" Frey managed to force out. Blood dripped down from the corner of his mouth.

"What's that? How do I know you? Well, you already know we come from the same place. We're both strangers to this new world. If that's true, then who does not know of the great Emperor? The man said to be chosen by God to raise his kingdom from the pile of shit it was, only to unite Earth under one flag!" the woman proclaimed with exalted laughter and threw up her arms in the air. She spoke with enthusiasm and genuine admiration, but there was a bitter undertone when she sat back down to continue speaking. "You, somehow, managed to make previous wars look like child's play. Quite frankly, if not you, there is only one thing that could be called monstrous: that'd be the power of you and your sisters. Entire armies, even the Great Alliance, proved powerless before you, all while the Imperial Army suffered virtually no casualties! If that is not terror at its core, I don't know what is!"

She took a break from her speech to fiddle around with the bolt wedged into his body. Each flick of her finger let out more blood through the cut that led to his heart. Frey's sight faded away.

"No, your power wasn't what was monstrous. At the very least, I don't think so. It all makes sense now, ever since I met my master. No, no-no-no! The only monster was *you*!" the woman said and raised her voice. Even when warped beyond recognition, her disdain for him was clear as day. "All the men and women, every soldier and leader, anyone who spoke out against you: slain without mercy or pity – like cattle at the slaughter! All the children who lost their parents, they meant nothing to you! They could have been spared, imprisoned; no one had to be orphaned! No one had to be left alone, wondering why their mothers or fathers never came home, why they could never hear their voice again! In your righteous madness, did you ever stop to think of that?!" she shouted furiously and slammed her fist in his stomach.

Frey could not respond. Too much blood had gathered in his throat and lungs, and he could no longer breathe.

"No. A tyrant as drunk on power as you could never."

The assassin stood back up and stepped over him in the direction of where Frey entered.

She stopped and said with her back against him, "I don't think you deserve it, but if it's any consolation: I don't know if your sisters have ended up here as well. My master mentioned no such thing. He just wanted you dead. Even so, I wouldn't go after them. The problem was with you anyway. It always has been."

Frey barely saw her walk away in the corner of his eye, completely paralysed – a situation he had already experienced once. The woman casually whistled a vaguely familiar tune as she left, although he could barely hear it. When she turned the corner and disappeared out of his sight, Frey stared up at the ceiling in darkness.

"*Is this it? What a cruel, twisted joke,*" Frey thought before he instinctively gasped for one last breath, only to breathe in liquid. Then, everything turned black.

Frey opened his eyes again. Now on his feet, he looked around, lost and confused. Still in the very same room, far below the surface, everything had lost its colour. The chairs, tables, even the chandelier were of a matte grey shade. Despite the lack of any light, he could see just fine.

"...*Am I dead? Is this death? No, that's not it... This isn't what happened the last time. Something strange is going on,*" Frey thought.

Frey turned to see his body on the ground, grey like everything else. He was too overwhelmed to notice anything other than the obvious scars, even the vague hint of light occassionally flickering in different areas of his corpse.

"*Is that me?*" Frey took his eyes off his body and looked down. His transparent uninjured chest, arms, and the rest of his body emitted a strange, orange hue.

Being the only thing of colour there, Frey's ghost-like form stuck out like a sore thumb.

"*This radiance... it's familiar. It reminds me of the souls I used to see. Then that really is my body?*" Frey glanced back at his corpse. For some reason, he felt calm. There was no anger and no grief, no worry or fear. "*Souls never had this kind of structure. They always appeared like some sort of energy, similar to how the Oracle described it, never in the image of their old self.*"

Though he had not noticed it himself, Frey was not quite the same. He stood much taller, his well-toned body completely unclothed, and his tied-up hair reached his lower back. Older in appearance, a difference most noticeable around his face, he appeared to be more in his late twenties.

Shadows in the form of a black cloud appeared in the middle of the room and pushed themselves up to create an oval shape.

"...Is that a portal? Who's there?" Frey said with a raised voice.

"A voice, here?" something replied; its voice was calm but raspy and echoed from all directions. It was difficult to know whether it truly came from the portal.

Doubt was erased when the end of a crooked stick slammed into the ground out of the dark cloud, followed by the owner. A black foot in the form of a bird's, larger than the size of a human's, stepped through. White talons donned the tip of each of the four toes that dug into the ground. Then emerged its avian head, covered in black feathers and with a sharp, shiny beak. On each side of its head were three deep, red eyes aligned along their head. What first appeared to be a stick was, in fact, a scythe with a rose-red blade. A three-fingered hand held it in a tight grip. Long claws made up half of each finger. The menacing figure stood tall and proud. Its head nearly reached the top of the high ceiling. Most of its body was covered in a garment the shade of a sunless sky with dots scattered all over its robe; they were twinkling like stars.

"Do my eyes deceive me: a soul the shape of a mortal? And it speaks and walks?" the creature said in great surprise, which then immediately turned into uneasiness. "Oh, I see… The essence that surrounds you. You are one of *them*."

Each of its six eyes stared at him intently; carefully, it examined Frey.

"*You*," Frey uttered. Wary of the creature, he distanced himself from it. "You are a Servant."

"Now *this* is a surprise. You know of us? Who are you, human? Why are you here?"

Frey scoffed. "Hmph, if only I knew that."

The unnerving creature narrowed its eyes.

Without taking his eyes off the Servant, Frey introduced himself. "Once, I went by the name William; that was in a world much different from Setura. Here, I am known to a few as Frey. Unfortunately, I did not get much time before I died at the hands of someone from my world. Who are you, Servant?"

"To speak with such a lack of respect when you are aware of my truth – I have never experienced anything like this before. I advise you, human: had it been someone else in my stead, your insolence would have been answered with your destruction," the Servant warned him.

"So be it. It has been long since I bowed my head in submission, even to the likes of your kind," Frey told him, unphased by their threat.

"Aware of our existence *and* our authority, yet you refuse to kneel?" the Servant exclaimed and threw their head back in laughter. "You intrigue me, human!"

"You have yet to tell me your name, Servant," Frey reminded them, indifferent to their entertainment.

"Ah, of course. It would appear my fascination with you got the better of me," the Servant admitted, still laughing.

They went silent. Then they tapped their scythe in the ground which sent a shockwave through the ground and caused the earth to quake. The chandelier swung around while dirt and dust fell through newly formed cracks in the ceiling.

"I am Raeven, the First—Primora Warrior of Erium. As decreed by my Lord, I alone care for the souls of Setura, to guide the deceased to their forever after! The mortals of His world revere me as the god of death!" it declared. Each spoken word caused the air to tremble.

"As I suspected. To appear here and now, it could only be a Servant to take care of the recently deceased. A First, nonetheless."

Before Frey could open his mouth, Raeven, having finished their introduction, continued to speak.

"I must say, your soul tastes like the other two I sensed before. I thought it was strange but no matter. You are undoubtedly the one who stood out the most," Raeven said and gazed off into the distance, though they subtly kept three eyes on him.

Frey's eyes widened ever so slightly. *"What did he say? The 'other two?' Could it be? Wait, I cannot afford to get ahead of myself. I won't give him any advantages,"* Frey thought, careful not to slip up. "What other two do you speak of?"

"Why do you ask?" Raeven questioned, already aware they meant something to Frey.

"Hmph, Servants are no fools. I'm sure Raeven mentioned the 'other two' on purpose to see if I knew anything of it. Undoubtedly, they noticed my soul's reaction. I shouldn't make this one an enemy – not yet," Frey thought and analysed the situation.

It was not the first time he had to deal with sly Servants. Aware of his disadvantage, Frey decided to tell Raeven some more of his situation in hope that the truth would be to his advantage.

"Fine, I will play along with your little game. In life, before I arrived in Setura, I had two sisters. In my world, we met our end at the hand of a traitor and her despicable plot." Frey paused, afraid to hope—if he could even experience it. Dead already, he had little left to lose. "Do you know if they are the other souls you mentioned?"

"As I thought. They *are* related to you," Raeven revealed. Frey's assumption proved correct. "Human, do you know how new souls are born?"

"Only human souls," Frey answered, having already taken a dislike to the Servant from their conduct. Although irked by them, he concluded that Raeven asked the question for a good reason and shared his understanding. "A sliver of each parent's soul is carried over to the unborn child. These slivers grow and fuse into one. As souls grow, they can develop emotions, personalities, and a sense of self. The ability to use magic also comes from the soul, which in turn depends on its parents. That is how it worked in my world; is it similar here, or does it differ?"

"It is not only similar. The reality is that it works precisely as you have described it. Now that I know that your understanding is at least greater than abysmal I can freely explain what it is you wish to know," Raeven said. Their condescension exposed their view of mortals.

"*Typical Servant,*" Frey thought, annoyed beyond belief.

Raeven explained, "When it comes to humans, the birth of a soul is the same for all. Humans who descend from the same two souls may think and feel differently from each other, but at their core, at the very heart of their souls, they carry an unmistakable resemblance to one another."

"You are saying it is them then?"

Raeven held off his answer. "You said you were killed, correct?"

"Yes."

"What about your sisters?"

"They… were also killed right before my eyes. It was the last thing I saw," Frey told him, his bottomless sorrow hidden behind a face of stone.

"Hm. Then it is likely to be as I have predicted," Raeven said and put one up talon to their beak. "Some time ago, there was a disturbance in Setura's aura. They occur from time to time—like ripples in a puddle on a drizzly day. However, that time was different. Instead of a droplet, it was a boulder. Although it is not uncommon for wandering souls to enter and leave our domain, you should know that it is rare for us to notice you. It must have been many mortal millennia since the last time something stirred up the ancient balance this way."

"We are the cause. Are you sure?"

Raeven sneered. "Do not insult me, mortal. Even my patience is finite."

Frey backed off, at this point unwilling to anger the god further. "Apologies, it was not my intention. Then, are we the first to cause this, well, commotion?"

Raeven remained silent for a moment. "No. No, you are not," they informed him with their crimson eyes fixated on the human. "You are not the only ones to have caught our attention. Usually, we do not interfere with mortal souls, except in death or when absolutely necessary. This was decided in our First Council."

"*The First Council,*" Frey remembered, *"made up of the oldest and usually most powerful Servants. Varius told me about them. They settle internal disputes or conflicts without the need to bother their masters."*

"This time our Council was in discord," Raeven disclosed.

"What, why?" Frey blurted out, surprised that the Council could not reach an agreement.

Raeven did not even pretend to think of an answer and instead ignored him completely.

"Out of the many souls I sensed then, three of them were nearly identical. One of them stood out like the Light in the sky – who I now see was you. If what you say is true, then there is no doubt about the other two. The resemblance, circumstances, and time of arrival leave no room for chance."

Frey was conflicted. Finally, he knew that they were there with him. It gave him a sense of relief to know that they had not simply ceased to be, that the three could still have reunited. Yet, he had to face the truth. He was already dead. Was it too late?

"No other Servant of Setura is capable of differentiating between souls of the deceased as I. No mortal can hide from my sight in the afterlife. The only other who might come close to my ability would be-, well, never mind." Raeven's eyes lit up. "This knowledge may be in our favour."

"What do you mean 'our' favour? What are you scheming?" Frey asked, distrustful of Servants as he always was. He knew better than most how similar Servants were to those they considered little more than insects—namely humans. Because of this similarity, they could potentially be great allies – or terrible foes.

"Rejoice, mortal! I have a proposal!" Raeven exclaimed.

"What sort of proposal?" Frey questioned their sudden, suspicious benevolence.

"I see the guilt and despair poorly tucked away in your soul. Your failures and your shortcomings: they can still be rectified. What if I told you that I can offer the chance to reunite with those you have lost, to be given a second life in Setura?"

"Spare me your trickery. I do not doubt your ability to return me back to the living. What is it you want in return?" Frey asked.

Raeven chuckled. "The truth is that tensions have risen between us Servants. Our master has left for a place where we cannot see, for a reason none of us know. We have been acting out our duties in accordance with our Council, but the integrity of it has begun to crumble."

Frey was stunned. "Is this true? I cannot believe a Creator would vanish just like that… Although I suppose that is not of my concern. Fine. What part do I play in this?"

"I have reason to believe that there is a way to reach Him. The issue is that my only clue lies somewhere in Setura. We are forbidden from walking the earth unless we are attending to our duties. Therefore, we are left with only one option: to patiently await His return," Raeven explained.

"Have I understood you correctly, Raeven: you want me to search for this way to your master in return for being brought back to life?"

"Precisely so."

Frey stared at the Servant, who steadily awaited his answer. The proposition appeared fair, but he was not so naïve as to blindly accept it.

"While your offer is decent, I have two conditions that must be met in order for me to make a decision," Frey told them, emboldened by a crucial realisation.

"Is that so? Name them," Raeven told him with sparked interest.

"My first condition is as follows: I do not become your subject nor you my master. This is an agreement between us as equals. You can grant me something I desire, and in return, I aid you in something no one else can. If this was not the case, I doubt we would have this conversation."

The Servant was left speechless by the sheer absurdity of his request: that they could ever be considered equal. After a few suspenseful moments, Raeven broke out into a raspy laugh; dark feathers scattered in the air.

"If you only knew how unbearably boring our menial meetings are in the Council! I have not been entertained like this in millennia! The inhabitants of this realm are truly incredible! Human, consider your first condition to be lunacy, madness, outrageous, and granted!" Raeven exclaimed in wild, unrestrained joy.

The sudden outburst from an otherwise gloomy god of death was an odd sight. Their previous laughter was little more than a chuckle in comparison.

"My second condition," Frey continued, indifferent to the Servant's enjoyment, "I will keep my end of the bargain and assist you in looking for your master. However, I will only do so after I find my sisters. I do not know if you are allowed to, but are you able to guide me to them? It would be in both our interests that I find them as soon as possible."

The Servant grumbled in deep thought.

"It has little to do with permission. *This*, us here and now, is a violation of our rules – let alone your resurrection. This," they said and swept their arm through the air, "should never have taken place. If the others discover what has transpired here, it will most certainly become a cause of concern."

"If it is not about permission, then what is it?"

"While the other Servants of Setura could be considered inept when it comes to the souls of the dead, my proficiency is limited. Just like yourself, your sisters have been reborn into the bodies of Seturan mortals – human, of course!" Raeven emphasised.

Frey had never considered the possibility that they might have not ended up as humans, though he felt relieved to know it was not the case.

Raeven continued. "That is an issue. As they now live, I am unable to find them."

"That… is disappointing. Is there no one else who could assist us?" Frey asked.

Raeven hesitated. "To find a specific mortal, lost in the Seturan ocean of souls, there is only one other Servant who could be considered my equal. Unfortunately, They will not help us. As it stands, we are on our own. Will this be a problem?"

Because no other Servant could be allowed to know what would be set in motion, Raeven feared Frey would take advantage of the situation.

"I believe it could be," Frey told him and scratched his head, unaware of their suspicion. "My abilities are not what they used to be, even my magic cannot be used to its full extent."

This caught Raeven's attention; their blood-red eyes lit up. "What do you mean?"

"A few days ago," Frey said and turned to Raeven, "a friend of mine was ambushed by a small pack of wolves. We almost died at that time. Not from the wolves but because I could not control my magic as I should have," he explained.

Raeven became more than intrigued by his story.

"Is that so? I can discover what went wrong!" Raeven declared with pride.

The Servant approached Frey and placed the tip of each clawed finger on the ghostly surface of his forehead. Frey drifted backwards when he suddenly found himself staring up at the ceiling.

"Am I back. Am I alive?" Frey thought. He could neither lift his arm nor turn his head. As he looked around, he noticed that the world around him was still void of colour.

The Servant's beak came into view as they leaned over him to inspect his body closer.

"Ah, yes," Raeven mumbled. "As you know, what permits you mortals to use magic depends on your soul. If it were not to be anchored properly to the vessel – which in your case is this frail, weak human body – it may have dire consequences."

"Explain," Frey's voice said, his thoughts echoed out loud.

"A loose soul may affect your personality, your memories, and magic. Unexpected death is also possible, though that is rarer," Raeven told him.

"So, that's what happened to me? That would explain everything."

"Correct. Your soul is acting erratically—desperately trying to break free from the confinements of your body. I do not know why."

Raeven's explanation reminded him of something he had heard just days before. *"Didn't the Oracle mention something similar?"*

"The Oracle?" Raeven asked as he continued his examination.

"Do you mind? These are my thoughts," Frey told Raeven, annoyed.

Raeven was amused. They leaned in closer, having uncovered something of interest. "I can sense traces of another soul beneath yours. How strange. They are oddly similar. What should normally happen when a soul is reborn is to merge with an existing, infant soul; the result can be quite interesting! However, sometimes the existing one is instead cast out for me to harvest. In your case, it was simply shattered, broken into many fragments."

Raeven was evidently disturbed by his discovery. It worried Frey.

"These scars, were they always there?" Raeven asked and scraped the surface of Frey's body with a single claw.

"No. I was told I had been struck by lightning. Apparently, that took place a week before I woke up in Setura," Frey answered.

Raeven scoffed. "Lightning? Nonsense. Whatever destroyed the soul also caused your wounds. This is troubling. *What in the Ravaged realms could have caused this, and how did this body survive…?*" the Servant whispered, perplexed by Frey's past.

"I see. So, are you saying these fragments were the reason why my magic went awry?"

"Precisely. They have prevented your soul from attaching properly."

"Can you fix it?" Frey asked.

Raeven fixed their eyes on Frey, insulted. *"Can I fix it?* Have you forgotten who you are speaking to? This is nothing!" the Servant boasted and then narrowed its eyes again. "However, before I do, there is something we must agree upon."

"I know. I have given you my conditions. Will you accept?" Frey told the Servant.

Raeven stood up. He silently thought over whether to accept Frey's terms. After some time, the Servant broke the silence.

"I will give you ten years to live your life as you please. If you succeed in finding them before your time is up, you may live freely until the final hour. On the contrary: if you have failed to find them, you must do what I need of you," Raeven told him. They noticed Frey's uncertainty when presented with the counteroffer.

"Ten years? Maybe it'll be enough time. I shouldn't underestimate the task at hand though..." Frey thought, having briefly forgotten his thoughts were not private at the time. "Ten years with no obligations: is that what you are offering?"

Raeven nodded their head in confirmation.

"Very well. I accept," Frey told them, neither thrilled nor upset with their agreement.

"Excellent! Would you do the honour?" Raeven asked, finally appeased. They offered Frey to reiterate the contract as a show of respect, where Frey would state the terms and conditions for Raeven to accept. This, figuratively, put them on equal footing.

Frey stared up at the ceiling; his sisters appeared in his mind. Though confident throughout their negotiations, he knew well the dangers that came when doing business with unpredictable deities. Still, he could not help but feel a sense of hope.

"I, Frey, recognise Lord Raeven, First of Setura, in this sacred bond. In exchange for my resurrection, I will assist in finding a way to your master, the lost Creator. Upon my revival, I will have ten Seturan years to live my life freely as I wish. This contract is established between equals!"

Frey's voice was loud and without fear.

"On my honour, as the First Servant of Erium, the only soul carer of Setura, as the fearful Last, and in the name of my master: I accept!" Raeven proclaimed, his voice caused the earth to tremble.

As soon as Raeven finished, Frey was suddenly pulled back out of his body, into the ground, and watched as Raeven faded away in the distance.

Chapter 5.

"Revival"

- - -

The summer sun shined down brightly on the wooded plains that made up most of the Enn forest. There were hardly specks of white in the clear blue sky for as far as the eye could see. Nothing would have been out of the ordinary if it were not for an odd lack of beasts roaming the woods—or the Spot.

High up in the sky, far above the forest of Enn, there was a dark blob the size and shape of a small black cloud. No one quite knew when it appeared. It did not move with the wind and had been growing for at least a couple of months. The Spot first caught the attention of local villagers and passing wanderers. Some feared it to be a bad omen while a handful of mages gathered to study it, believing it to be some sort of natural magical phenomenon.

One day without warning, when the sun stood at its highest, the ground directly below the Spot erupted. A pillar of darkness broke through the surface and sent an earth-shattering shockwave through the soil. The midday sun vanished as night fell over the land. The pillar soon faded away; all that remained in the blue was the figure of a man, clad in dark clothes with a long, bladed weapon in hand and something otherworldly on his back.

Frey gasped for air as if he was suffocating. Sweat formed; it dripped down his face and into his eyes.

His body was clothed in an exquisitely soft, grey fabric, lined by deep purple details. His chest and lower legs were protected by dark steel metal plating while his hands and forearms were covered by smoky metal sheets held in place by leather straps. A strange, dark hooded cape covered his shoulders and back down to his feet. It waved unnaturally in the wind.

"W-w-what the hell? Where-. Light? That's… the sun. A-am I… back? Is this real? Am I… finally here?" Frey thought, confused and agitated with a scythe in his right hand, identical to Raeven's. He took a few much-needed moments to calm himself down and slow down his breathing. It took a while until his eyes stopped searching for something to appear—or rather for signs of Setura to disappear at any moment. What could be the reason for his strange behaviour?

Eventually, Frey began to look around and then down, where he saw a massive crater in the middle of the forest.

"What? Did I do that? How– when?" Frey stared at the mess he thought to have created.

As Frey surveyed his surroundings, his mind still in a state of disarray, strands of silver-grey hair waved before his eyes. Hesitantly, he reached out to grab hold of it with the tip of his thumb and index finger. His hair, the colour of the moonlight, was long and silken smooth.

Unsure of what to think or feel, Frey put his thoughts aside when he noticed a flapping sound that came from behind him. A pair of wings sprouted from his back with feathers dark as Raeven's.

"Whoa-whoa-whoa!" Frey exclaimed in shock.

The wings moved wildly out of rhythm to each other; each flap sent him flying. As the initial shock passed and he calmed down, he began to gain control over them, and sure enough, his wings stopped thrashing. With the wings under control, he stepped down onto an unseen surface.

"These… are mine?" Frey mumbled, bewildered by their sudden appearance.

They moved through his will, and the one on his right wrapped around to the front. He dropped the scythe, which remained floating in the air, and reached out his hand to grab hold of his new feathery appendage. To him, they appeared to be that of an angel, only black as the night. He softly ran his fingers over the pinions and stared at them as if he refused to trust it could be true.

"They're... not gone," Frey stated after some time. "Then... this is all real?"

Frey looked around at the green. He spied at the glowing light of souls of the critters and creatures in the forest, fleeing, with purple glowing eyes. Although still among the clouds, everything appeared as if he was right there in person. The light faded away and his vision returned to normal. He took a deep breath and inhaled the fresh air and then noticed how stiff his body was. After stretching his limbs, back, and neck, he exhaled.

"I'm back - not a damned moment too soon. How long was I gone...?" Frey thought and stared at his wings. "I admit that I've missed flying but really? Well, now I see how Katja and Lynn got used to theirs so fast. They're not *that* strange. I shouldn't be complaining," he remarked. Though not least bit alien to the idea of bewinged humans, he certainly did not expect to wake up with a pair himself.

The light in Frey's eyes died out and he stared off into the distance as the faint, hollow lamentation came creeping up and grew louder in his ear. His head twisted upwards and he began to gasp for air as his eyes shut tighter the longer it went on. With a quick jerk, he snapped back to reality. He exhaled while reminding himself not to listen. "First... that nightmarish place; then my hair; followed by these clothes and scythe; and now *wings*? What the hell happened?" he asked himself, frustrated and lost.

His thoughts were interrupted by the flap of his left wing. With his hand still resting against the right one, he began to seek answers. "*I can feel my hand touch it. Every feather I tug on feels like pulling on a hair. Is this some sort of spell? No. No, this is not a conjuration or an illusion. This can only mean...*" he thought and looked up. He closed his eyes and sensed an ancient, powerful magic flow around and through his body. When he opened them again, he gazed up at the unnatural night sky. "Primordial magic."

The luscious grass and shrubbery, every creek and river, even the white-topped mountain peaks in the horizon, turned stone grey as their colours faded before Frey's very eyes. The wild winds died out in an instant, and the wandering clouds in the distance came to a halt. Frey's body and the scythe hovering next to him retained their colour.

Shadows gathered in front of him to form a massive, oval shape. Raeven stepped out. This time, they appeared much larger and were met by a smouldering Frey.

While initially astounded, the Servant soon became deeply concerned. "Well, this was certainly not expected. I sensed something had happened; no doubt the others felt it as well... What happened here? How did you invoke this power?"

Already distressed as he was, Raeven's question sent him over the edge. "You are asking *me* that?! *This* is your bloody doing! *You* did something to me, and I demand you tell me," Frey told them, furious, and then shouted, "now!"

Frey's hand cut through the air in front of him and unintentionally sent out a shockwave that flew past the Servant and into the distant mountains. In the heat of the moment, he failed to recognise the power he used.

The Servant said nothing. Instead, they scratched their beak in thought. "Hm," Raeven mumbled, having assessed the situation. "Aside from beginning to mend the soul fragments together with your soul, I had to replace your heart. There was something... problematic, shall we say? The projectile embedded in your body; it had begun-."

"The... what?" Frey asked, confused.

It was not until Raeven reminded him of what had happened that it came back to him, though only as vague pieces.

"I-I… Right… Right, y-yes, I remember," Frey stuttered. He squinted, desperately trying to remember more but without much success. "Was… wasn't it a simple poison-covered bolt?"

"It was anything but simple," Raeven told him. "There was a powerful curse placed on it – a curse not of this world. I was forced to use my power to dispel it to prevent the rest of your soul from being destroyed and to replace your destroyed heart. However, I would never have guessed *this* would happen as a result."

Frey went silent when he saw a massive crater appear in the mountains and pieces of it fly behind the Servant, both a result of his shockwave. He also remembered that before Raeven's appearance, he spied on the creatures in the Enn forest despite being so far away. Then he finally realised it. He knew there was only one reason to why Raeven's Primordial Magic had resulted in him regaining access to his power. He stared the Servant dead in the eyes.

"Raeven, I believe I know the answer."

"Do tell."

"As you know, my soul and those of my sisters were unusual, to say the least. I do not know if you were already aware of this, why they stood out to you. The truth is they entered soul pacts with two Servants of our world," Frey told him. Part of him questioned whether he had made the right choice.

Raeven could not believe it. "What?! No, that cannot be true!" they exclaimed in utter disbelief and pointed their scythe at Frey. Furious at such an outrageous claim, they shouted, "Do not dare lie to me again, mortal!"

Frey remained still, indifferent to Raeven's threat—not so much because of fearlessness but rather because it was the truth.

"I did not lie."

"What mad Servant would do something—with a human no less?! Who could possibly allow it?!"

Frey shook his head, disappointed by the Servant's tantrum. "The elder of my two younger sisters, Catherine, bonded with Cyra. The other with Zev."

Raeven's eyes widened. A dark aura surrounded their scythe. With one swing, it flew at Frey. The dull side of the blade phased through his clothes and armour and came to a halt when it touched his skin.

"You… It is true?" Raeven said after a few seconds and lowered their weapon. "Cyra and Zev. I cannot believe it. So, that was the taste I recognised. It was different, yet I knew something was familiar. Their master is-. No…" The Servant's eyes pierced Frey; their body trembled when a truly disturbing possibility dawned on them. "You did not?"

Frey knew Raeven understood and nodded. "Yes. I bonded with Varius."

Raeven's grip weakened, and his scythe plummeted to the ground.

"Varius the Elder? It cannot be. Even among our Masters, Varius was there before most. His wisdom was a guiding light after the wars. How, how could he do something so foolish – dangerous?!"

It took a few moments for the shock to settle – a feeling the Servant thought themselves incapable of or perhaps simply had forgotten.

"How could Lord Varius allow this to happen?" They looked up at Frey. "Did he lose it? Did he become… mortal?"

Frey shook his head. "I do not know."

"Human, you said you and your sisters were killed. Through the pact, you share the same fate. If one dies-."

"I know," Frey interrupted. "I have not heard from Varius since my death," Frey told them, aware of what his first death may have meant.

Dejected, Raeven lowered his head.

"Inconceivable. After all this, Lord Varius, dead? *Does my Master know?*" Raeven whispered to himself. They raised their head, determined to press forward. "Everything makes sense now. What I sensed earlier in your soul was Varius' Primordial essence. Although I vaguely recognised it, I never would have assumed it to be. That very essence, it absorbed mine, which I used to save you. Because of this, you have changed."

"You mean the wings?" Frey asked and glanced back at them.

"They are now a part of you, but it was not what I had in mind," Raeven said and swiped their hand in front of themselves.

Black mist gathered and dispersed to leave behind a mirror. Given the complete lack of them in Delera, this was the first time he had a chance to see his reflection which was not on the surface of the water. Frey stepped closer, and his eyes widened.

Visually, he remained largely similar to before his second resurrection. However, he had grown a few years and gone through some notable changes. His dark hair is now moonlight silver and reached down to his shoulders. His eyes, which were once oak brown, had become stormy grey. Frey leaned closer to inspect his face and caught a faint amethyst glimmer in his eyes before it faded away. It was as if time itself had been rewound, and he could not stop staring.

"That's me...?" the young man asked himself, astonished by how alike the two were. He looked away from the mirror and to the Servant. "I did not do this, Raeven. Is it what I think it is?"

"It seems that your soul used the Primordial magic to reflect its image onto its vessel, changing your eyes and hair in the process. Perhaps, if given enough time, you would have completely regained your old appearance."

Both were equally surprised by how unpredictable Frey's resurrection turned out to be.

"It seems we were similar in mind and body, Frey," he whispered to his reflection. "You said you had to recreate my heart?" he asked Raeven and placed two fingers on his neck where he felt a strong pulse.

"I had no choice. You were cursed by a powerful spell. Death was unavoidable, but it would not have been the end. It would have eventually destroyed you. Had I taken any longer, you would be no more. What you feel now is not the beating of your heart."

"Then what is it?"

Raeven recalled their weapon in an instant and placed its wooden tip on Frey's chest.

"A gem, finely crafted to replace what has been lost," they explained and then lowered their scythe. "Since I did not have the time to completely destroy the curse, I made this crystal heart to continuously release Primordial magic and suppress it. It is a perfect substitute. You should feel no difference."

Frey's eyes wandered to his chest, and he pulled down his shirt. There was new scar tissue where his old heart used to be.

"*After all this time… I'm back,*" Frey thought and exhaled deeply. He turned to the Servant. "I am alive?"

"Indeed. Because of my magic and your replaced heart, I can easily find you, even though you are alive. This is beneficial to us both. However, new dangers have surfaced," Raeven said with great concern. "You have inherited some of Varius' essence through the pact. You, as a mortal, cannot freely benefit from our power."

Frey knew well what Raeven referred to. "*There's*

always something, isn't it?" He sighed, more annoyed than anything. "Yes, I am aware. Varius actively repressed the Primordial magic so that it would not overtake me. Cyra and Zev did the same for my sisters. However, that was then. I am not sure what to expect here."

"I am impressed you resisted its corruption, even with Lord Varius' aid," Raeven complimented him, though who could guess whether they truly commended or simply belittled him?

"Am I at risk here?"

Raeven stood still and mumbled to themselves as they scrutinised him with glowing red eyes. "I am observing your soul as we speak. Unfortunately, it would seem as if it has already begun to spread. I believe it is due to your current state. Can you revert it?" Raeven asked without expecting too much.

"I can try."

Frey closed his eyes. The Primordial magic was a force like ravenous rivers rampaging inside his body. While it granted him power, it also consumed him.

Before he knew it, Frey found himself face to face with a luminous silhouette of a human body in a vast emptiness. It gave off a brilliant shine in a display of all the rainbow's colours. Within the light there was a pulsating deep violet radiance surrounded by a still darkness. While staring at it in wonder, captivated by the beauty of a soul, he noticed strands of light cut through the darkness. They were sucked into the gem and further spread the darkness around his heart.

As Raeven mentioned, the Primordial magic pouring into his soul had already begun its corruption. Though the force was neither good nor evil, it overtook what could not resist.

"If left as is, Setura will overwhelm you. Cyra, Zev, and Lord Varius protected you from your world's Everforce for a reason. However, I need to know you can stop it on your own, mortal," Raeven's voice echoed in the dark.

Frey could not allow the gem to absorb Setura's ambiance – the Everforce. There was no room for failure. Though, to resist it was no different from trying to swim against the current. It was a near impossible fight. Fortunately, his past experience came into hand.

"*Although Varius prevented it from taking me over, he only intervened when it got close in doing so. I don't think I can stop it, but could I redirect the flow? Maybe that's possible?*" Frey thought.

His efforts appeared meaningless at first, but Frey persisted. He kept manipulating the Everforce, little by little, as it began to flow past the hungering gem rather than to pour straight into it. The night faded away, and the sun's rays started to shine down on the ground below. Frey's wings broke down into a dispersing mist.

Eventually, when enough of the Everforce had been redirected away, Frey managed to create a vibrant orange barrier around his Primordial heart. When day returned to Setura, Frey opened his eyes.

"Excellent, mortal. Your control is praiseworthy. I suppose I should have expected no less from someone who bonded with Lord Varius."

"Is that all it takes to impress you, Servant?" Frey replied with a smug look on his face.

Raeven disregarded his pride. "Your vanity aside, after watching you, I am certain. Lord Varius' gift to you absorbed my essence in the gem. As a result, you have gained some of my power. As to how much and to what extent, only time will tell—if you survive."

"I cannot afford an 'if,'" Frey told them, determined to succeed in his task.

"What a curious thing: Primordial magic in a mortal's body," Raeven remarked, though they did not sound surprised. "You have changed drastically over the past year that you have been asleep."

"Hold on, a year? It's only been a year? No… No, I was gone for much, *much* longer," Frey said in a mellow voice as if he were ready to fall asleep. Dread came creeping up his back.

"What do you mean?"

"I… I'm not sure," Frey mumbled. "Thinking back to it, my memories are all one hazy blur, but… I remember a vast emptiness and torn-up skies. All I could do was walk and walk and walk. It felt like an eternity, and no matter how far I went, it never ended. It was bleak and cold, and it reeked of death," Frey told them, uncertain whether what he remembered was real or not.

Raeven remained silent but took a subtle step back. They braced themselves as if something terrible were to happen, while Frey appeared unaware of their strange, sudden apprehension.

The more time that passed, the clearer certain memories became. "I think the first thing I tried to do was to count the days, but day never came. I tried to count the steps it took to walk between two points, just so I would not go mad all alone, but the distance was always different. I remember people wailing with no one else there. The very last thing I remember was when I sat down by a tree of stone. I heard someone speak. Who was it again, a woman? I don't remember what they said." For an instant, Frey dropped his formal, albeit sleepy voice. Instead, he spoke softly and with affection. With a delicate, tired laugh, he told them, "I don't remember them, but it felt warm."

A few moments of silence passed where Raeven stood petrified and Frey stared into the Servant's cape with empty eyes, as if he was entranced.

"I blinked, and the next thing I knew I was here," Frey said and looked up to the Servant. It was only then he noticed Raeven's odd behaviour, clueless as to what was wrong. "Are you– Is something the matter?" Frey asked, confused.

Raeven kept eyes on their vicinity, watchful of something neither seen nor felt. They then regained their composure and shook their head. "No, it is nothing." Raeven cleared their throat. "To address your experience: it sounds to me like you have lived through the Ravaged realms."

"Is that where I was? I am afraid I am only familiar with the name," Frey told him. "Does it all look the same?"

"It depends on the Servant. From what you have told me, there is no doubt you were in my domain, the Nocturnal Wastes. That is to be expected, though I did not anticipate your soul to remain conscious," Raeven explained and added that this was likely due to Varius' essence. He still remained guarded.

"I figured as much. A lot of time passed there… Far more than a few years."

Raeven shrugged. "We do not share your concept of time. A thousand years on Setura could be a day in the Ravaged realms and could just as well be ten thousand years. Our home is nothing like you have ever known before."

"Yes, thank you. I noticed," he remarked sarcastically. "What about the voice? Was it someone sent by you to bring me back?"

Raeven shook his head again. "I sent no one as your body was not yet ready. About the voice, I have no answer. It is entirely within the realm of possibility your mind simply could not endure the stay," Raeven told him and dismissed his questions as mere figments of imagination.

"Ah…" Frey mumbled, disheartened for an unknown reason. He ignored his emotions. "You know, I spent a long time there – alone. There were times I doubted what was real and what was false, even when it came to myself," he said in a toneless voice as he stared out at the greyed-out landscape. He paused only to then glare up at the Servant. "After so much time, perhaps longer than it should have taken, I was beginning to believe you had tricked me."

"I would do no such thing!" Raeven scoffed at the very thought.

"I never said you did," Frey told them. Raeven narrowed their eyes. "Besides, there is something else on my mind: our agreement. You said I have been gone for a whole year?"

"It could not be helped. Unlike what it must have been in your previous life, this body of yours was rather weak. Not only did it have to adapt to sudden usage of magic, but it also had to survive the curse and my essence. I had no choice but to let you heal," Raeven explained.

"Yes, yes, I understand. What about our contract?"

"Hmph, I am not unreasonable! Our contract states you had ten years to *live*. Naturally, they begin now."

Frey sighed out of relief. *"These are good news. Finally, I can begin. I don't know how long my search will be. I would've hated to lose a tenth of my time just like that..."* he silently reflected while scratching his chin. He looked the Servant in the eyes, bowed slightly, and placed his closed fist against his left palm in front of his chest – an ancient show of respect towards a senior, a senior Primordial being. "Allow me to express my most sincere gratitude. I have met my fair share of Servants who valued trickery and dishonesty over what was right, simply for their amusement."

"Save your gratitude. There was nothing I could do to hasten the process," Raeven replied with little regard for Frey's gesture. "There may be the need for us to work together soon. Planting the seeds of distrust now would only poison our relations in the future."

"Regardless, you have my thanks."

Raeven paused. "The Primordial corruption has stopped. I believe I can see your soul recover as well. This is good news," they said, content with the situation.

Frey was not quite as worry-free. "The rate at which it spreads is concerning. I did nothing out of the ordinary and used no Primordial magic," he caught a glance of the mountain behind Raeven. "Err… well, almost no magic. I will need to be careful going forward."

Raeven nodded. "Your judgement is accurate. With that said, you will be able to use our power rather freely in this form, but exercise caution when doing so. The use of Primordial magic will make it spread. The more it does so, the longer it will take for your soul to recover. For now, I see no immediate danger."

"How will I know when to stop, when it spreads too far?" Frey asked, accepting of any advice the Servant may have for him.

"It is difficult to know. I suspect it will first strain your body, though I do not know in what way. Unfortunately, I cannot be much of use to you."

Frey casually shook his head. "You have done enough already. I will handle the rest on my own."

"What will you do now?" Raeven asked, curious of what he may have planned.

"I will not sit around and waste time. I must find my family. I worry they may be more incapacitated than I was."

Raeven nodded. "Your worry is well placed. As you now know, the consequences of a loosely attached soul vary greatly. I would only know what would happen for certain if I saw it myself. Of course, by then, it would be too late."

Frey could not bear the thought to lose them. However, as much as he longed for their reunion, there was something else that he felt compelled to do.

"There is nothing more I want than to see them again, but there is something I must do first," Frey said and spoke through his teeth.

Raeven sensed his fiery emotions.

"And that is?"

Frey frowned at the Servant. "Are you aware of humans capable of peering into the future?"

Raeven laughed. "It is only thanks to our benevolence that you have that ability! Yes, every now and then I encounter their souls. Why do you ask?"

"To the humans of Setura, they are known as 'Oracles.' I consulted a young one before I ventured off on my own. I asked her to see into my future, and the vision brought me to that cave," Frey explained. Anger built as he thought back to his death.

"You believe this so-called Oracle lured you into a trap?" Raeven asked.

"That is the truth I intend to unearth. My assassin is someone from my world. And from the way she spoke, I fear that she was also in contact with a Servant of Setura."

Raeven's eyes shot open. "This is an alarming discovery. We are not to interfere with souls reborn into our world, dead or alive. The Servant who guided the hand of your assassin knows this well. Did she mention who it was?" Raeven asked, greatly disturbed to hear another of their kind had also secretly intervened with a mortal.

"No, I do not know who she or her master is. My only lead is the Oracle."

"Tell me," Raeven said and moved in closer – Frey thought himself to have seen a sinister smile somehow creep up on Raeven's beak. "What will you do when you find this Oracle?" they asked with eerie interest.

"If she had *nothing* to do with this, then that is what I will do," Frey told them.

"And if she *did*?" the Servant insisted, searching for a specific answer.

"If she did… If she was aware of what she was doing and willingly lured me into this trap, then you may soon expect a little gift from me," Frey answered, his words coated in blinding wrath. Having suffered one betrayal after another, he succumbed to his emotions.

Raeven eyed Frey in silence, only just able to contain their laughter. Their entertainment was complete, for now.

"Very well," Raeven spoke up, "I am putting a great deal of faith in you, Frey. You carry the essence of the Eternal within you – divinity! Few are those able to stand against you. However, remain vigilant. If another Servant has already attempted your life, I am certain they will seek you out once more."

"I will not allow anyone to stand in my way," Frey replied and firmly grabbed hold of the scythe that had been floating next to him. He examined it for a second before he tossed it up in the air where it dissolved into nothingness. "With all due respect, that weapon was not for me. I prefer something I am more used to."

Frey reached out his hand where shadows converged to form an elongated shape. The darkness dispersed to reveal a beautiful sword. The blade itself was made of a beautiful, dark metal, and its grip was wrapped in black leather. A single glistening, blood-red ruby laid embedded in its crossguard. He swung it around and noted its weightlessness – much like his armour, cloak, and clothes.

"*It'll take some time to get used to it, swinging a sword with no weight. I wonder why it's like this. Never once have I conjured something using Primordial magic. Never needed to. Strange,*" Frey thought as he grazed his palm against the blade's edge only to cut through both his cloth and flesh without effort. The wound closed up, and the cloth regrew nearly instantly.

"Primordial magic is far different from the lowly magic you are used to. Creation, simple or advanced, is no task. Anything created remains until destroyed. I would highly advise not to attempt meddling with the living. The risk of the strain placed on your soul is far too high," Raeven cautioned him.

"Objects are fine then?"

"As I said, avoid the living," Raeven answered, annoyed his petty question.

Frey let go of his sword, which vanished immediately, and spread his wings out from his back. "I believe I should be on my way, Raeven. I have a life to live and certain people to find. Thank you for your help."

"It was nothing! Ah, but before we part ways, I have something important to tell you! With some luck, it might aid you in your search," Raeven hinted.

"And that is?"

"A few centuries ago—or was it millennia? Regardless, some time ago, I met with some humans. I bestowed upon them the greatest gift any mortal could desire: immortality. Apparently, conflict broke out between them and other humans. Though not dead, they are in hiding. If you can find them, you may be able to convince them to your side."

Raeven's advice was met with scepticism. "A 'gift' you say? And how would I find them?"

Raeven laughed and opened up the portal of darkness once more. "That is for you to figure out! Clear your mind and follow your instinct. Be cautious around the Seers, lest they sense your heart," they said as they drifted through the portal. Once through, it vanished.

Colour returned to the world, and the distant clouds resumed their gentle travel through the skies. The sun's rays warmed Frey's body even when so high up.

"*Sense the connection – you have it too,*" Raeven's voice whispered.

Frey rolled his eyes. "How typical of Servants to always give half of the important information. They really do as they please. What a pain…" he muttered, only to sigh when he realised his childish behaviour. "It is what it is, I suppose. Still, I can't believe I never realised how useful Primordial magic could be. Although it has no limits, it turns out that I do. As for Raeven's strange behaviour… something wasn't right, but I think ignoring it was the right choice at the time. I can't afford to make him my enemy."

Now, before proceeding with anything else, Frey needed to become more accustomed to his wings. Although they were in truth no different from his arms or legs, at least when it came to being part of his body, he had to teach himself how to use them. With some time and a great deal of patience, as he reached them outwards and back in, he eventually managed to move them in what could almost be considered unison. Then with a single, forceful flap of his wings, he shot up high like a bullet.

His eyes glowed purple. "Let's see… That over there should be the Snowcrown mountains – east, I think," Frey mumbled as he surveyed the land and threw an eye at the noon sun. He faced west. In the distance, he saw the weak glow of countless souls through the earth and trees. "And that… Ah, I see you, Siria."

Thinking there could be a need to conceal his identity, Frey reached out his open palm away from him. Shadows gathered and dispersed to leave behind a dark mask with a red outline of a single eye on the right half. Even while equipped, his vision was unobstructed.

"Now, I do believe it's time for me to pay a dear old acquaintance a visit," Frey said in a heavily distorted voice. With a flap of his wings, he sent himself gliding through the air straight toward the big city.

Copyright ©
All rights reserved.

Twitter: @AFallenCrown

Made in the USA
Las Vegas, NV
21 January 2022

41984332R00088